Plank Road
Summer

Plank Road Summer

by
Hilda and Emily Demuth

CRICKHOLLOW BOOKS

Crickhollow Books is an imprint of Great Lakes Literary, LLC, of Milwaukee, Wisconsin, an independent press working to create books of lasting quality for young readers.

Our titles are available from your favorite bookstore. For a complete catalog of all our titles or to place special orders:

www.CrickhollowBooks.com

Plank Road Summer
© 2009, Hilda and Emily Demuth

This is a work of fiction. The characters are drawn from the authors' imaginations, and any resemblance to actual persons living or dead is coincidental.

Cover artwork is by Kathleen Spale.
www.kathleenspale.com

Original Trade Softcover

Publisher's Cataloging-in-Publication Data
(Prepared by The Donohue Group, Inc.)

Demuth, Hilda.
  Plank road summer / by Hilda and Emily Demuth.

  p. ; cm.

  Includes bibliographical references.
  ISBN: 978-1-933987-06-4

1. Racine County (Wis.) – Social conditions – 19th century
– Juvenile fiction. 2. Plank roads – Wisconsin – Racine County
– Juvenile fiction. 3. Hotels – Wisconsin – Racine County
– Juvenile fiction. 4. Fugitive slaves – Wisconsin – Juvenile fiction.
5. Wisconsin – Fiction. 6. Hotels – Wisconsin – Racine County
– Fiction. 7. Fugitive slaves – Wisconsin – Fiction. 8. Historical
fiction. I. Demuth, Emily. II. Title.

PS3604.E48 P53 2009
813/.6

To Mom

with fond memories
of our Plank Road days

Acknowledgments

We are grateful to our respective households–Mark P. Lutze, Katrina, Elena, and Matthew of Hil-Mar Farm, and Y. Franklin Ishida, David, Hans-Martin, and Louisa of Spring Rose Cottage–for their enduring love and patience when we "snuck away to write."

We give thanks to the Demuth clan, especially to our mother and our late father, Marjorie and Robert Demuth, for a lifetime of love and support. We appreciate the advice and encouragement of Don Driscoll, Elizabeth Hunter, Julie K. S. Moyer, Rich Novotney, Julia Pferdehirt, Rhonda Telfer, Teri Witkowski, and the Elmhurst book club.

Many thanks to Dick Ammann of the Racine Heritage Museum, to Kathy Borkowski and Kate Thompson of the Wisconsin Historical Society Press, to writing instructors Laurel Yourke, Kathleen Ernst, and Jerry Apps, and to the Lilly Teacher Creativity Fellowship program.

We appreciate the work of our editor, Philip Martin, and the volunteers and staff at Wade House, Pendarvis, Old World Wisconsin, Stonefield Village, Milton House, Oak Clearings Museum, and Graue Mill, who treated us like authors long before we had a book.

Contents

Prologue

From the Racine harbor on Lake Michigan, the road ran west, through the oak clearings of southeastern Wisconsin, seventy miles to the Rock River. Once this gently rolling land had been the domain of Indians and trappers, who left little trace of their passage over forest and prairie. Now, homesteads with pastures and wheatfields made a green and gold patchwork of the clearings between vast groves of great burr oaks.

Along the dusty or often-muddy road, eastbound wagons carried the bounty of farms to the harbor on Lake Michigan. Westbound travelers brought longed-for news and supplies deep into the heart of Wisconsin.

One summer day in Yorkville Township, a little brown-haired girl sat on a farmhouse porch. Swinging her bare legs back and forth, she watched the planking of the road that ran past her farm.

Along the newly graded roadbed, oxen stood patiently, as teams of men unloaded rough-cut four-by-four "stringers" from the wagons, laying the timbers end to end in two long, carefully parallel lines. Across the stringers, the men placed eight-foot planks side by side to make the road's platform.

All day, the pounding and voices of workmen echoed across the Yorkville farmyard, as the brown-haired girl sat and watched.

A quarter-mile west of the brown-haired girl's farm, a small cabin stood among the oaks. Closer to the roadway, the framework of a large new building, a two-story country inn, was under construction. Within those invisible walls, a little fair-haired girl with a basket sat and watched the planking of the road, till a woman's voice from the cabin summoned her inside.

By sunset, when the work teams had moved west to the next homestead, a golden path, smelling sweetly of fresh-cut lumber, lay between the small cabin and the neighboring farm: the smooth, inviting surface of the Racine and Rock River Plank Road.

Chapter 1

Blossoms

Plunging into the prairie grass, brown-haired Katie cut across the green wheatfield for home, leaving the schoolhouse behind. She arrived in the farmyard red-faced and panting, her sunbonnet dangling on her back and her dinner pail bumping against her skirts. Along the embankment of the plank road that bordered the McEachron homestead, her oldest brother Will was walking heavily, halting to stomp his boots every few steps.

"What are you doing?" Katie asked.

"Tromping down these wheel ruts," said Will. "See where a wagon veered around the tollgate? Must have come tearing through here well after dark. Sneaked through without paying the toll."

Katie wrinkled her brow. "It's not harvest. Why would anybody travel by night?"

Will shrugged. "I wonder that myself. We need to get rid of the tracks so nobody is tempted to follow the path of a shunpike. Any more such incidents, and Pa or I will have to sleep in the tollhouse."

"I'll help you tromp," said Katie. "I'm in a tromping mood."

"That's not a good way to come from the first day of summer term."

Katie stamped the sides of the rut. "All Miss Waite would

say is 'Not now, Katie' or 'Keep still, Katie.'"

"You do have a way of bursting out."

"You never minded when I spoke up. You were a much better teacher than Miss Waite."

Will grinned. "I hope you didn't express that sentiment at the schoolhouse." He tromped the last rut smooth and headed off toward the barn.

Katie frowned. When she heard the jangling of harness bells and the sound of hoof beats, she looked down the road. The approaching wagon was passing the Mather Inn, where Katie's best friend Florence was already pulling sheets from the clothesline. As the wagon neared the tollgate, Katie crossed the dirt lane and clattered across the plank lane to the tollhouse. She hoped that her sister Matilda had not heard the bells.

"Katherine McEachron!" cried Matilda from the porch, with an emphasis on the -eck, "You know you're not to take toll!"

Matilda arrived on the run at the gate just before the teamster pulled up his horses. She pushed Katie aside, then said, "The toll is five cents, sir" so sweetly that Katie rolled her eyes.

The driver touched his broad-brimmed hat. "*Guten Tag,*" he said. He reached into his vest pocket and handed Matilda a half dime. Before Matilda could turn to swing the gate, Katie stepped to the pivot block to push aside the long wooden arm that blocked the wagon's passage. As the gate swung open, the teamster clucked to his horses, called "*Auf Wiedersehen!*" and continued his journey.

Katie followed her older sister into the tollhouse. "May I mark the ledger?"

"You're just a schoolgirl." Matilda set aside a worn brass bell that lay on the open ledger, then took pen in hand to record the team's passage. "Remember, a mismarked ledger cost the old gatekeeper his job." With slow precision, she signed her name on the line beside the word *Keeper.*

"Where'd you get that bell?"

Matilda placed the bell carefully on the ledger. "A teamster gave it to me."

"What teamster?"

"One who can speak English." With a little smile Matilda turned toward the door. "Ma needs you to help with supper. Grace is coming tonight."

"Ma never used to make a fuss over Grace Caswell. Why is it different, now that she's to marry Will?"

"You're too young to understand." Matilda left the tollhouse before Katie could think to respond.

Reluctantly Katie trudged across the road to the farmhouse.

She was nearly at the porch when she heard Ma's voice: "Katie, how was your day?" Ma was digging a plant from the fragrant wall of lilacs that hedged the backyard.

Katie pretended not to hear the question. "Is that Grace's lilac?" She peered at the clump of heart-shaped leaves. "Why don't you choose a better one? That one hasn't any blooms at all."

Ma smiled. "'Tisn't blossoms that keep a young plant strong. With good roots and plenty of water, this one will bloom beautifully next year."

"White blossoms, I reckon," said Katie, breaking a sprig from a nearby bush. "You always give white lilacs to brides. And purple ones for new things, like babies and houses. Like when the toll house got a purple lilac."

"Do I?" said Ma. "I never thought of it. But I *am* digging a white lilac for Grace."

"I tried to tell Miss Waite about the lilacs, but she is not a very good listener."

"Shouldn't *you* be listening to Miss Waite?" said Ma. "Change your apron and start peeling potatoes for supper. I'll be along directly."

Katie sighed and took a whiff of the lilac in her hand. "Everybody asks about school, but nobody really wants to hear what I have to say," she said to herself as she crossed the porch to the kitchen.

Most of the talk at the dinner table that evening was about making Will's new house on the east forty acres ready for a bride. Ma and Matilda offered Grace advice about curtains and cookery. Will talked to Pa about expanding the orchard between the new house and the homestead. Thomas and Amos, Katie's brothers closest to her in age, one older and one younger, argued over the best location for the henhouse.

After supper Katie took the broom from the corner and began sweeping the dining room. Through the wide doorway to the front room, she could see Pa reading in his rocking chair and Will recording the day's events in his farm journal. Thomas, who had finished school last winter, was repairing a harness. It seemed to Katie that his mind was always on horses.

She carefully swept around the legs of Amos, her schoolmate, who had settled at the dining table to begin his schoolwork.

At the other end of the room, over the clinking of dishes, she heard Grace in the kitchen say, "My Gran says every house in Yorkville has a lilac bush from the McEachrons."

"When we left New York State," Matilda said, "Ma made up her mind to bring her lilacs with her to Wisconsin Territory. Pa said we hadn't room enough in the wagon, and Ma said, 'If you left your books behind, we'd have room enough.' Then Pa said, 'Without books, a house is not a home,' and Ma said, 'Without lilacs, a house is not a home.' Somehow they found room enough for both."

Amos looked up from his slate. "Katie was talking all about lilacs in school today."

From the front room Pa called, "And how was the first day with the new schoolteacher?"

Katie kept sweeping. She said quickly, "Miss Waite doesn't allow us to ask any questions."

"She's new to the position," said Pa. "What sort of questions did you ask?"

Amos began to tick off the questions. "Miss Waite, may I get a drink of water? Miss Waite, will we run out of room for stars on the flag? Miss Waite, do you know about the lilacs in Yorkville? Miss Waite, do you think you'll ever get a white lilac?"

Katie glared at her brother. "I can't help it if Miss Waite dislikes my inquisitive mind."

Ma came into the dining room from the kitchen. "Perhaps you misunderstood something she said."

Amos snorted. "How could she misunderstand 'Go stand in the corner'?"

The rattling of dishes in the kitchen stopped. Thomas looked up from the harness, and Will paused, pencil in hand. The rocking chair gave a creak in the silence as Pa rose. "Katherine, come with me."

Katie leaned the broom against the wall and followed him into the study, where a narrow desk stood against one wall opposite a tall bookcase. Pa sat down at the desk and nodded toward the chair in the corner.

"What happened at school today?"

"It wasn't fair of Miss Waite to punish me."

"Did you speak out of turn?" Pa's voice was crisp.

"I didn't mean to, Pa. But we read a poem about lilacs, so I had to tell about Ma's—"

"Did Miss Waite punish you for speaking of lilacs?"

Katie lifted her chin. "When Will was schoolmaster, he never minded when I had my say."

Pa raised his eyebrows. "Is that what you told Miss Waite?"

"No, Pa. Not exactly. I just said she'd never be as good a teacher as Will."

At her father's stern expression, she added, "It's the truth, Pa. Shouldn't we always speak the truth?"

Pa sighed. "You have been taught to speak the truth. But you've also been taught to respect others, especially those in authority. Surely you understand that what you said was wrong."

Tears welled up in Katie's eyes. "Sometimes I can't help what I say. The words come out so fast, Pa. By the time I remember not to say anything, I already have."

Pa leaned back in his chair and stared at the wall. He was silent for so long that Katie followed his gaze to the broadsides, the posters tacked beside the desk. Below the license that proclaimed Andrew McEachron to be a justice of the peace hung the toll fees for the Racine and Rock River Plank Road Company, next to an advertisement for the A. P. Dutton warehouse in Racine. A crisp new poster listed the penalties for violating the Fugitive Slave Law.

Katie wondered what her own penalty would be for her latest episode of getting into trouble at school.

To her surprise, Pa lifted the lid of the desk and took out a small book like the ones in which he and Will kept their journals.

"Katherine, the Scriptures tell us that there is a time to speak. And a time to keep silence. Perhaps if you practice 'having your say' in these pages, you might better be able to keep silence when your words could hurt others."

Katie wiped her cheeks with the back of her hand. "You're punishing me by giving me a book?"

"Tomorrow you will apologize to Miss Waite."

"Yes, Pa."

"And on Saturday you will do extra chores."

"Yes, Pa."

"And you will not cause any more disruptions at school."

"No, Pa."

Pa opened the little book to the flyleaf, wrote two lines, and dried them with a blotter before handing her the opened volume. She read in his neat script, *To my daughter Katherine in her 13th year, 1852.*

"Pa, do you think I'll ever recognize a time to keep silence?"

He put his work-worn hand over hers. "On a farm, we know that anything is possible between blossoms and harvest."

Later that evening, after Will left to walk Grace home, Katie slipped out to the porch. The scent of lilacs filled the evening air, and the last rays of the setting sun fell across the marbled cover of her journal. She opened the book to the first page and began to write:

May 10, 1852

Pa gave me this journal because I spoke disrespectfully to Miss Waite on the first day of summer term. I will try to recognize a time to keep silence, as Pa says.

But how am I ever to know exactly when that time is?

Chapter 2

Quilting Day

In the kitchen at the Mather Inn, just down the road from the McEachron farm, Florence pushed her blond braids back over her shoulder. Then, she began to arrange cinnamon twists on a platter. Her mother was frying potatoes at the wood-stove, while her grandmother sat with her morning tea at the little table by the window.

"Look, Florence, will 'ee?" Gran Mather was peering into her tea cup. "I see stems amidst the leaves. A dark stranger is coming."

Mrs. Mather turned, skillet in hand. "A fine inn we'd keep if nary a stranger, dark or otherwise, showed his face."

Florence said, "What manner of stranger? When will he arrive?"

Gran shook her head. "I cannot tell, only that with him comes a shift in the wind."

"Florence, don't 'ee mind such Old Country nonsense," said Mrs. Mather. "Gran, I wish 'ee'd remember we're not in Cornwall."

Gran smiled and smoothed her lace cap. "We're Cornish all the same."

Florence carried the platter to the dining room, where a burly man, a teamster whose wagon was a frequent sight along the plank road, sat with two other teamsters and a farmer and his young son. The burly man took two doughnuts before passing the platter down the long table. "Now you'll have a rare treat," he told the farmer's boy. "From Janesville to Racine and back again, you won't find cinnamon twists like those of the Mather Inn."

The platter went round the table, and Florence saw the cinnamon twists disappear two at a time. Reaching for a third, the teamster said to the farmer, "You'll want to watch for broken planks outside Burlington."

"I saw a work crew out that way yesterday." The farmer wiped crumbs from his beard. "Fine stout oak they had aboard that wagon."

The teamster chuckled. "The great men of the Plank Road Company should have known to start with Wisconsin oak, instead of Michigan pine." He turned to the farmer's boy. "And what sights have you seen on your journey?"

The boy swallowed a bite and gulped his milk. "I've been to the harbor, sir," he said, his eyes alight. "I've seen the sea."

"Not the sea, Jacky," said the farmer. "Lake Michigan."

"The greatest of the Great Lakes," said the teamster. "The goods we haul to that harbor will travel all over this country and to lands beyond."

The porch door creaked as Florence's father entered the dining room.

"Tell me, John Mather," said the big teamster, "where's that long-faced fellow who gave you such a time last night? No appetite this morning?"

Mr. Mather smiled. "Do 'ee remember how he wanted me to knock down the price for his stay? Said he'd take no whiskey nor feed for his team. This morning what do I find? He and his horses gone, leaving a trough full of nails where they'd been."

"Nails?" said Florence. "Who would put nails into a feed trough?"

Mr. Mather chuckled. "In the dark, our clever friend must have reached into another wagon and grabbed what he thought was a feed bag. I never before met a man who couldn't tell nails from oats."

The men around the table roared with laughter.

That afternoon, under the great oaks between the inn and Gran's nearby cabin, Florence set seven chairs around a quilting frame. On the little table borrowed from the kitchen, she set a cream pitcher filled with purple lilacs.

"Florence! Florence Mather, where are you?" The voice came from halfway across the sloping pasture on the McEachron land. Red-faced and panting, Katie was running just as hard toward the inn as she had run away from the schoolhouse the other day. Charging into the oak grove, she gestured toward the approaching buggy and gasped, "I told Mother I could run faster than Thomas could drive!"

The McEachron buggy turned off the road and swung into the yard, Thomas and his father up front, Amos in back, wedged between the billowing skirts of his mother and Matilda. Pulling into the inn yard just moments later came the wagon of the Mathers' neighbors to the west. Big Jim Doane and his wife Sarah sat up front with their two grandsons, Silas and Daniel, behind in the wagon bed.

"Look, Florence, the Doanes have a new horse!" said Katie, hurrying toward the inn yard.

Florence followed more slowly, glancing back to see that the chairs had been placed according to her mother's directions.

Mr. Mather stood at the watering trough, greeting the guests. He nodded toward the strapping chestnut horse harnessed to the Doane wagon. "That's a fine beast, James," he called. "Put him to plow, will 'ee?"

Big Jim Doane grinned as he eased himself from the wagon. He ran a huge hand down the chestnut's foreleg. "The good Lord never intended these to walk before a plow."

Mrs. Doane snorted. "I didn't know the Almighty was in the habit of confiding His intentions to you." As the little boys climbed down from the back of the wagon, she fixed the older one with a stern look. "Now, Dan'l, you look after Si," she said as the two trotted off toward the barn.

Under the oaks Florence helped Mrs. McEachron, Matilda, and Katie pull the top of the patchwork quilt tightly across the frame.

Mrs. Doane said, "The squares have come together right nice. There's nothing prettier than a Bride's Album quilt."

Each square was different. Florence ran her fingers carefully over the oak leaf on the square Gran had made. Mrs. McEachron had stitched the schoolhouse, and Matilda had embroidered a golden sheaf of wheat.

"See my lilac?" Katie said, "I wanted to make it white, but Ma said that wouldn't show on a white background. I had to make it purple with green leaves." She traced the outline of Florence's square. "How cleverly you made the Mather Inn."

"That was Mother's idea." Florence tried to brush aside the memory of her mother's scoffing at her first notion of a square depicting a Midsummer fire.

The women and girls set to their afternoon's task, carefully stitching along the faint scrolling lines marked by Mrs. McEachron. Mrs. Doane said, "Elizabeth, you've done well in this match. You couldn't ask for a finer daughter-in-law than Grace Caswell. And it don't hurt that the Caswell land adjoins your own. I reckon Will heeded his mother's advice in choosing a wife."

Florence wondered if anyone might choose to do otherwise than to heed a mother's advice.

Mrs. McEachron did not break the steady rhythm of her needle. "William has worked very hard on the east forty," she said. "He and Grace are making a garden today."

Matilda looked up from her corner of the quilt. "The way Will talks about that place, one would think he and Grace were going to live in the Garden of Eden."

Katie giggled. "Except they won't be naked."

Florence blushed, and Mrs. Mather frowned. But Gran and Mrs. Doane shook with laughter. Mrs. McEachron shook her head. "Katie! That will do. And Matilda, you need not speak so lightly of Scripture."

Katie and Matilda made faces at each other across the quilt. Gran said cheerfully, "I must take Grace some cuttings for her kitchen garden." She turned to Mrs. McEachron. "Tell us about the wedding plans, will 'ee?"

"After the service and the wedding dinner for kinfolk at the Caswells," Mrs. McEachron smiled across the quilt at Mrs. Mather, "we intend to invite everyone in the township to a wedding dance at the Mather Inn."

Katie bounced with excitement, but Florence just sighed. For Katie, the wedding day would be time for feasting and fun, with a procession down the plank road and an evening of dancing. But Florence foresaw long hard hours ahead. Mrs. Mather prided herself on running the cleanest inn around. If she insisted on spotless floors and gleaming windows for a few weary teamsters, what would she demand when all the settlers in Yorkville were invited to enter that front door?

At a sudden shriek from behind the cabin, Mrs. Doane said, "Katie, will you see what Dan'l and Si are up to?"

Instantly Katie put down her needle. "Yes, ma'am!"

"I'll help," Florence said, starting from her seat.

"Sit 'ee down," said Mrs. Mather. "There's work to be done."

As Florence sank back into her chair, Gran said to Mrs. Doane, "Faith 'n' truth, Florence has such a neat hand I can't tell where my stitches leave off and hers begin."

The women worked in silence for a short time before Mrs. Doane said, "Matilda, should we be planning another Bride's Album quilt? Isn't it time Owen Caswell started building a house of his own?"

Matilda blushed and bent lower over her sewing, her eyebrows drawn together in a frown.

"When Matilda and Owen have anything to tell," said Mrs. McEachron, "surely we'll be the first to hear. Sarah, tell us more about the plans for the fair. To think that five years ago Wisconsin was not even a state. Now we are ready to hold a Racine County Fair."

Mrs. Doane settled in her seat. "Jim and I have offered use of our land for the fairgrounds. What do you think of that, girls? We'll have this grand exhibition on our own front forty!"

Mrs. McEachron smiled at Florence. "How well I remember the fairs back east. Imagine over a hundred buggies and wagons lined up along the road. All the townships send the best they have to offer. Jams and pies and quilts and I don't know what all. Folks bring their finest livestock. And you'll see every color of cattle and fancy breed of poultry. The men talk of nothing but horses, of course."

Mrs. Mather's mouth opened and then closed quickly. Florence knew she was pondering the effect of such a momentous event on the inn. Florence sighed, silently calculating the number of hours she might spend frying cinnamon twists.

Chapter 3

Around the Inn

K atie found the little Doane boys in the log barn where the Mathers stabled the horses and oxen of their guests. Silas was sitting in an empty stall whimpering and clutching his arm. Daniel stood over him, arms crossed. As Katie knelt beside Si, she heard a sharp hiss from under the feed trough. A calico cat lay curled in the straw, her kittens squirming around her.

"I told him not to touch 'em!" said Daniel.

With an edge of her pinafore, Katie dabbed blood from the long scratches on Si's arm. "We'd best wash you up," she said. Scrambling to her feet, she hoisted Si to her hip and carried him out to the yard, Daniel trailing behind her.

Mr. Mather and Big Jim Doane were standing near the watering trough looking at the new horse, and Thomas was at the chestnut's head, stroking his muzzle. As Katie dipped a corner of her pinafore into the water and pressed the cloth against Si's arm, Big Jim said, "We'll have a fine track if we start near the road and sweep out past the lone oak. It would make for a grand race."

"And have 'ee just the horse to enter?" said Mr. Mather with a wink at Thomas.

"Mark this, John Mather. On this day you beheld the winner in your own yard."

Thomas grinned. "I'd like to see Lightning in action," he said, "but I reckon I'd best get home to mind the gate." He gave the chestnut a final pat and returned to the buggy, where old Rowena stood short and stout alongside the long lean chestnut.

As the buggy pulled out of the yard, Katie set the Doane boys to floating leaf boats in the watering trough. When a call from Ma summoned her, she returned reluctantly to the women gathered around the quilt. Matilda's red-gold hair shone in the dappled light under the oaks, and Mrs. Doane's laughter rang out across the yard. Florence and Mrs. Mather had their heads down, intent on their work, but Gran Mather looked up and smiled as Katie took her place again in the circle.

All through the afternoon, Katie quilted dutifully. Her legs were cramped and her fingers ached, but she was pleased when Ma praised the evenness of her stitches. The delicate scrolling stitches linked all the squares, including her crooked lilac, into the landscape of the Bride's Album. Still, Katie was glad when the Mathers left the quilting to start supper. When Mrs. Mather rang the great dinner bell, Katie started from her seat immediately.

Ma shook her head. "Lavinia is just calling the men over. We've time to finish the edging before they arrive."

With a sigh Katie rethreaded her needle and returned to her task, trying to ignore the tantalizing aroma of ham and molasses. It seemed forever before the buggy pulled into the yard, Thomas at the reins with Pa beside him and Amos in back.

"There," said Ma with satisfaction. "Won't Grace be pleased? Help me roll this up, girls, and we'll pack it in the buggy."

Matilda was staring across the pasture. "Look, Ma, there's a wagon coming. I'll run home to collect the toll."

"You needn't, dear. We'll send Thomas back."

But Matilda was already on her feet, hastily gathering her skirts, cheeks flushed and eyes bright. "I can run faster than

Thomas can drive."

Katie watched with astonishment as her sister bounded over the section-line road and charged down the slope toward the tollgate.

From the inn's kitchen door, Mrs. Mather called, "Florence, bring in the chairs. Katie can help 'ee."

One by one the girls carried the chairs back into the inn and set them around the long dining table. As Katie carried in the last chair, she glanced out into the yard and stopped in her tracks. "Florence, look—Matilda's riding in a teamster's wagon!" Leaving the chair in the doorway, she bolted outside to the porch where Pa and Mr. Mather stood.

The driver halted his team at the watering trough and stepped down from the wagon. He said something to Matilda that made her smile and shake her head.

A whoop and a holler split the air as a big black horse galloped into the yard. Raising a cloud of dust, Charlie Doane took a spin around the yard before pulling up sharply. His sons Daniel and Silas squealed with excitement.

"Matilda McEachron!" called Charlie. "Who's your new beau? Does Owen know you're out driving with a dark-haired stranger?"

Without a word, Matilda hurried up the porch steps past Katie into the inn.

Daniel and Si were clamoring for their father. Big Jim lifted them into the saddle, Si onto his father's lap and Daniel hanging on behind.

"I'd best get these young'uns home," said Charlie. And while little Daniel whooped, they careened out of the yard.

Big Jim eyed the golden sorrel tied behind the wagon. "Mighty fancy horse for a teamster."

"I'm David Banvard of Rochester," the teamster said.

"I drive for Richard Ela." He turned to Mr. Mather. "I'd be obliged, sir, if you'd put me up for the night."

Thomas and Mr. Doane had moved in close to the sorrel, a mare who put her ears back along her flaxen mane. "Touch of lameness?" said Thomas. "She favors the right foreleg."

The teamster nodded. "Twisted it the other day."

"Let's have a look," said Big Jim. He slid a hand down the golden sorrel's chest. "Look at the length of those legs." He squinted up at David Banvard. "She as fast as she looks?"

The teamster's blue eyes crinkled in his thin face. "She gets me there on time."

Mr. Mather tilted his head to one side. "Katie, will 'ee be so kind as to tell my wife we'll be having another to supper?"

In the kitchen Mrs. Mather was poking at the fire in the woodstove. When Katie gave her Mr. Mather's message, she straightened up and pushed back a damp tendril of hair. "Florence, make ready the little room next to the stairs."

Katie followed Florence to the narrow back stairs.

Upstairs, Florence pushed open the window and tightened the ropes on the bed frame. She turned back the coverlet on the bed and lifted the ironstone pitcher from the washstand.

"Oh!" cried Katie, her voice coming from the large room that took up most of the second floor. "Look at the ballroom!"

Over the expanse of shining planks, the evening sun streaming through the windows painted four long stripes of gold. Katie spun over the floor so that her skirts flew out gaily, and a cloud of dust speckled the shafts of light. Reaching out her hands to Florence, she said, "Dance with me!"

Florence stood clutching the pitcher. "Oh, Katie, there's work to be done."

"There's always work to be done. Come and dance."

Florence glanced toward the stairs, then set the pitcher on

the floor and joined hands as Katie sang:

> *Camptown ladies sing this song,*
> *Doo-dah, doo-dah!*
> *Camptown racetrack, five miles long,*
> *Oh, doo-dah day!*

Together they pranced down the long room together, heels clattering like hoofbeats on the plank road.

At the chorus Florence joined in at last.

> *'Gwine to run all night!*
> *'Gwine to run all day!*
> *I'll bet my money on the bobtail nag,*
> *Somebody bet on the bay.*

"Katherine McEachron!"

The girls whirled to face the doorway, where Matilda stood with her arms crossed. "Florence, your mother wants you in the kitchen."

Florence picked up the pitcher and hurried down the stairs.

Katie stretched out her hands toward her sister. "Dance with me?"

Ignoring her, Matilda walked across the room and peered out one of the long windows. In the yard below, the teamster was currying the sorrel mare, whistling as he swept the brush over the golden back. When the teamster turned his face toward the inn, Matilda drew back from the window.

"What did he say to you?" Katie said.

"You're too young to understand."

The setting sun glinted through the windows in the dining

room when Mrs. Mather placed her guests around the long table. Gran Mather sat at one end and Mr. Mather at the other. Mr. Mather asked the blessing. As she bowed her head, Katie caught a glimpse of David Banvard staring at Matilda.

Big Jim Doane cleared his throat. "Tell me, Banvard," he said. "Meaning no offense, what's a teamster doing with such a horse as that sorrel?"

The teamster smiled down at his plate. "Pure fancy, I reckon," he said. "That's what I call her. Fancy."

"And do you fancy racing her?"

David Banvard shook his head. "I'm not much for a contest."

Mr. Mather began to pass around the platters. "Tell me, Banvard, how is business in Rochester?"

"Growing steadily. I deliver farm equipment, especially Mister Ela's new fanning mills. I make regular runs between Janesville and Racine."

"I hear there were slave catchers in Janesville a fortnight ago," said Big Jim Doane as he helped himself to another slice of ham. "Did they catch any fugitives? Did anyone collect a reward?"

The teamster answered slowly, "I've seen plenty of slave catchers up and down the Rock River. And the marshals are doing their best to uphold the law."

Gran clucked her tongue. "Imagine a poor soul traveling so far to escape slavery and then being hunted down in the free state of Wisconsin. How shameful."

Big Jim Doane smiled. "Meaning no offense, Gran," he said, "but you Cornish don't quite understand the way this country works." He turned to the teamster. "I was born in Kentucky myself. I know firsthand that black folks are needed in the South. They belong there."

Katie put down her fork. "But *you* left the South. Why shouldn't they?"

At Pa's stern look, Katie picked up her fork and began to eat her beans.

Mr. Mather said, "That's a fair question. I can assure 'ee I'd rather have teamsters than slave catchers on my property."

"You Cornish are all alike," said Big Jim. "I hear Old Man Caswell took up a collection on behalf of abolition."

Mr. Mather nodded. "A month back, the circuit rider preached on the Apostle's words to the Galatians, *in Christ there is neither bond nor free.* After the service, Caswell said 'twas his Christian duty to put money into the hands of those who work to break the chains of slavery. Then he passed around his hat."

Katie could not help herself. "Mister Mather, did you put money into the hat?"

"Hush, Katie!" said Ma.

Mr. Mather said, "Caswell said he'd take a hot iron to any slaver who came sniffing 'round his smithy. He said no man has the right to interfere with his property."

"And that's the very heart of the matter," said Pa. "Hard as it may be for Northerners to understand, in the South a slave is considered property, no different than forty acres or a horse. The slave owner would agree that no man has the right to interfere with property. And the law of this country is now on the side of the slave owner."

Ma shook her head. "Who would have thought that slavery would become an issue even in Wisconsin?"

"I don't see any issue," said Mrs. Doane. "People who mind their own business needn't worry about slave catchers or a midnight knock on the door. It's only the meddling folks who come to grief."

"The Maker keep them," said Gran Mather in a whisper, almost to herself.

As Mrs. Mather entered from the kitchen, Gran added cheerfully, "Sit 'ee down, Lavinia. Florence and I will bring in the pies."

After the Doanes left and the McEachrons were saying their farewells, Katie slipped out to the log barn with a scrap of ham. In the dark stall, she sat in the straw and listened to the kittens mewing and the mother cat gnawing at the meat. Then she heard footsteps and saw the swinging arc of an approaching lantern.

Mr. Mather and David Banvard entered the barn. The men walked to the far end where the horses were stalled.

The teamster said, "Mister Ela said I should ask what you might say to the prospect of a midnight parcel. Your inn is well placed between Rochester and Racine."

After a long silence Mr. Mather spoke. "Tell him that I would do all in my power to see such a parcel safely delivered."

The arc of the lantern swung past Katie into the darkness of the yard.

May 15, 1852

Midnight knocks and midnight parcels. What does all this talk of "midnight" this and that mean? Pa talks like a justice of the peace, but I wonder what he truly thinks of a law that is so unfair to the slaves.

How I hate to keep still at the dinner table. 'Tis like being a slave myself.

My fingers ache so from stitching that I can hardly hold this pencil. But the Bride's Album quilt did turn out right well.

Chapter 4

On the Road

Florence gripped the reins firmly as her father helped Gran up onto the wagon seat. "Easy now," she said to the gray workhorses.

Duke and Duchess tossed their heads and set their bridles to jingling, eager to set off. In the back of the wagon were two large baskets of pasties, the hearty pies favored by the Cornish. Under the seat were a stout oak staff, a basket, and Gran's satchel. Often Florence and Gran would "go a-gathering" herbs, filling their baskets with sprigs and roots and blossoms.

Florence knew how widely respected Gran's powers were among the settlers. Rarely did Yorkville families need to summon a doctor from Rochester or Burlington. Gran delivered their babies, cured their ills, and eased their suffering.

Gran never charged for her services—she always said she was "just being neighborly." Yet a day or two after a visit from Gran, a relative of the ailing one would show up at the inn with a pair of plump hens or a length of carded wool.

"G'dup!" Florence called, easing the reins over the broad backs. With a clanking of harness and a creak of the wagon, the team swung into a smart trot across the yard and onto the planks.

When the wagon approached the tollhouse, Katie came flying up to the tollgate. "Five cents, if you please!"

Gran chuckled as she reached into her drawstring bag. "And when did 'ee go on duty, miss?"

Just as Gran was about to drop a half dime into Katie's palm, Matilda appeared at the kitchen door. "Katherine McEachron!" came the familiar cry. "You know you're not to take toll!"

Matilda hurried out to the tollgate, wiping her hands on her apron. "Good morning, Gran. Good morning, Florence." Gran gave her the coin, and Matilda pushed against the counterweight to swing the gate.

Katie grinned up at Florence and Gran. "You'd think I'd be allowed to take toll from the neighbors! Going to Ives Grove today? Will's already gone to the smithy. Won't ever take me with him." She scampered off to the barn with a wave to Florence. "See you Monday!"

As the gate swung open, Duke and Duchess started up, and Florence loosened the reins to extend their trot. How she loved to hear the rhythm of the hooves over the planks, as each turn of the wheels took her farther from her household chores.

The wagon overtook a yoke of oxen, and Florence steered left off the planked lane to pass the slower-moving vehicle. Next a heavy wagon full of goods approached, and Gran signaled Florence to pull off onto the dirt lane.

"'Tis the way of the road," Gran said. "We are to ease the journey of those who are burdened."

At a narrow bridge two miles east of the inn, Florence pulled up the team at Gran's request. She picked her way down a slippery bank and dug several plants from a stand of iris. Last summer, she and Katie had spent an afternoon exploring this creek, following it from the McEachron back forty. How startled they had been to push through the reeds and come upon the bridge and the plank road.

Florence sighed as she hoisted the basket up into the back

of the wagon and climbed back into the seat. Since last summer Mother had given her more chores to do and less time to read and explore.

"Blue flag!" Gran said with satisfaction when she saw the clumps of iris. "Well done. I've a mind to try it on the Widow Everett's latest ailment."

Two miles later Florence could see the Ives Grove tavern, three stories towering above the crossroads. Several wagons were lined up along the hitching rail. Teams of horses were drinking from the great trough alongside the well. A tall man in a long dusty coat stepped off the porch. He took off his hat as he approached the Mather wagon. "Good morning, ma'am, miss," he said. "I'm Charles Carter, United States Marshal."

"I'm Brigid Mather," said Gran, accepting the marshal's help from the wagon.

"Of the Mather Inn?" said Marshal Carter. "Have you had any night travelers of late, ma'am? Any fast wagons come through? Folks behaving strangely about their loads?"

Gran's eyes went wide. When she spoke she sounded so timid and unlike herself that Florence turned to stare. "Why, faith 'n' truth, Marshal, I'd have called in the law if we had any such goings-on. I can't think what a decent body would be doing out after dark. The devil's business, I've nary a doubt."

"Yes, ma'am," said the marshal. "I'm sorry to trouble you about it." He nodded and returned to the porch.

Florence followed her grandmother up onto the porch. The men, holding their hats politely, made way for them. Florence walked through the doorway next to the dirt-smeared store window. Even before her eyes adjusted to the dim room, she could smell coffee and cinnamon, soap and beeswax. On the shelves above the long counter stood jars and tins and barrels of dry goods.

Mr. Ives came out from the kitchen in back, mopping his shiny head with a dirty apron. "Morning, Miz Mather, young miss," he said. "I'm hoping ye've a wagon load of yer famous pasties. My cook up and married on me, and I'm a sight handier in the barroom than the kitchen." He poked his head back through the doorway. "Henry! Get out to the wagon and bring in Miz Mather's pies."

One of the stableboys slouched through the store and out onto the porch.

Gran gave her list to Mr. Ives while Florence looked about the store. She saw a table strewn with unwrapped bolts of calico, tangled lace, and spilled jars of buttons. Mr. Ives sighed. "Looks like a magpie's nest now, don't it? Party of Norwegians come through, fresh off the boat. Jabbering and pawing through all my goods."

Gran looked squarely at him. "Many of us recall our time as foreigners in this land." She glanced over at the table. "Florence, set that corner to rights, will 'ee?"

When the stableboy returned with two baskets, Gran said, "Now, Mister Ives, I've marked the savories and the sweets, and I've made a dozen of the mixed."

"Ye are the salvation of me, Miz Mather," said Mr. Ives. He made a show of scooping extra sugar into the paper bag on the scales.

Florence rewrapped the bolts of cloth and stacked them tidily. She arranged the bolts by color, taking pleasure in the contrast of the calicos, sky-blue against crimson. She lined up the button jars and rewound the laces on the cards. From under the table she saw the end of a length of ribbon. She had to stoop and reach far into the dusty corner to find the spool. She began to wind the wide white ribbon, until she came to several smudged and well-trodden yards. "Mister Ives," she said, "what ought I to do with this soiled ribbon?"

The storekeeper shook his head. "Ah, that's fairly ruined."

"All it needs is a good scrubbing," Florence said. She was surprised to hear the echo of her mother's voice in her own.

Mr. Ives looked round his store with a grin. "Seems unlikely to happen here, don't it?" he said. "Young miss, ye take that ribbon home and scrub it to yer heart's delight. Go on, take the whole spool."

Florence blinked at this unexpected gift, then breathed "Thank 'ee, sir." She helped Gran carry the last of the packages out to the wagon, which Mr. Ives had loaded with sacks and barrels.

In the next moment, the daily stagecoach came rumbling down the road toward the tavern. Florence watched the Ives Grove tollgate swing open, and a team of four horses pulled into the yard. The driver tossed down the mail sack. As one man led away the lathered horses, a fresh team was backed smoothly into the traces. The reins were handed up to the driver. The driver swept his hat grandly to Florence and cracked his whip. With a lurch that must have flung the passengers into one another's laps, the coach bumped back up onto the plank road and clattered off toward Janesville.

Mr. Ives began taking letters and parcels out of the mail sack and calling out names. Florence was about to cluck to the team when Mr. Ives called, "Miz Mather, would ye be so kind as to take these on to the Yorkville smithy?"

Gran held the little sheaf of letters as Florence urged the horses out of the yard onto the north territorial road. On the dirt road, the hoofbeats were dull thuds instead of the smart rapping of hooves over planks, and the wagon jounced over the ruts as Gran leafed through the mail. "Letters from Cornwall for the Vyvyans and the Shephards. The McEachrons have a parcel from New York. I see that Alton Caswell is still getting his abolitionist society papers." She tucked the letters into her satchel under the seat.

A few miles later Florence saw the cluster of houses near the Methodist chapel. She pulled into the Caswell yard, where several children were playing in the grass near the spring.

At the wide doorway of the smithy, Charlie Doane and Will McEachron stood with their hands deep in their pockets. In the shade of a nearby oak, Becky Waite—"Miss Waite," as Florence called her now as the schoolteacher—and Pearlie Everett were seated together on a bench. From inside the smithy Florence could hear the ringing of the anvil, where Owen Caswell was singing a rollicking chorus in perfect time with his hammer.

Miss Waite and Pearlie Everett hastened over to the wagon. Pearlie said, "Gran Mather, is it true that Matilda McEachron was gadding about with a teamster? Charlie says he saw her riding down the plank road as bold as could be."

Gran smiled. "From the toll gate to the inn. Not even a quarter mile."

Old Man Caswell had left his job at the bellows to come and greet the visitors. At sixty, Alton Caswell could no longer swing a smith's hammer. His grandson Owen now worked the forge.

"And how's the prize scholar of Yorkville?" he asked Florence. "Is it true 'ee wore out Old Master Will and had to find a new one?" He winked at Miss Waite.

"Once he takes a wife, the old master will learn some hard lessons himself," said Charlie Doane. Pearlie giggled, and Miss Waite blushed.

Will smiled. "I couldn't ask for a better teacher than my Grace."

Florence reached back into the wagon and cut the stems

from the muddy bulbs of blue flag. As she stood holding the deep-purple iris, Old Man Caswell said, "Florence has her grandmother's eyes. What did Abel say of them? 'Eyes as grey as a storm at sea.'"

"I'm pleased 'ee remember those words," said Gran.

"Ah, Brigid, how would I be forgetting the only man in Cornwall whose wife could rival my own? Now come 'ee in, Esther is waiting."

Owen Caswell appeared in the doorway, his ruddy face aglow under a mop of curly brown hair. His shirt was darkened with sweat under the heavy smith's apron. "Good day, neighbors!" he called. "I'll be in directly."

Gran looked at the abolitionist society circular still clutched in her hand. "Alton," she said abruptly, "I want a word with 'ee." Old Man Caswell followed her across the yard to the little spring.

Will opened the gate to the kitchen garden and said to Florence, "I'm to join you for tea. Grace said I'd best learn Cornish ways if she must learn to be a Yankee wife."

Alton Caswell's wife, Gran Caswell, greeted them at the door. When Florence offered her the cluster of iris, she said, "What a dear 'ee are!" and kissed Florence soundly on the cheek, then placed the flowers in a porcelain vase beside her best teapot.

When Old Man Caswell and Gran Mather returned from their walk and entered the dining room, Gran Caswell brought in a platter of scones, a dish of strawberry preserves, and a bowl of clotted cream.

Owen arrived a few minutes later, his face and neck still damp from a vigorous washing-up. He nodded toward the blossoms. "I always know when Florence has come." He laid a handful of iron hooks in front of Florence. "What do 'ee think of my latest work?"

Florence picked up a wrought iron piece, admiring the heart-shaped back and holes for hanging. "It's lovely."

"Grace would be pleased to have a row of them in her new kitchen," said Will.

"I've a mind to sell them at the county fair," said Owen.

Gran Caswell smiled. "Mind 'ee make a few for us at home first."

"Now, Will," said Old Man Caswell as he heaped clotted cream on a scone, "have 'ee given up the scholar's life to become a farmer?"

Will smiled. "Our finest American writer tells us that there is virtue in the hoe and the spade for learned as well as unlearned hands. A farm, according to Ralph Waldo Emerson, is a 'mute gospel.'"

"A mute gospel . . ." Florence's mouth silently formed the words. "Where did Mister Emerson write that?"

"In one of his essays," Will said. "I know you've read some of his verse, Florence. If you would like to try his prose, I'll send the book by way of Katie."

After Will left for home and the Caswell men returned to the smithy, Florence and Gran said their farewells and went to pay their last call. They made their way to the churchyard behind the chapel. This lone acre, with scattered groups of white gravestones, was shaded by maples and sheltered from the winds by a row of small pines. Honeysuckle and the first buds of wild roses spilled over from the surrounding hedgerows. Gran took Florence's arm as they walked through the grass.

Florence knew not to talk to Gran in the graveyard. It was their place for remembering. Florence's memory only went back as far as her grandfather's burial here. But Gran had attended each of these funerals, had stood solemnly next to the very first graves dug on this land. She knew all of these names and their stories, the men and women who had died thousands of miles away from the places they had first called home.

Florence and Gran came to their own family plot. The tallest stone was carved *Abel Mather, b. 1790, Mullion, Cornwall. d. 1846.*

Florence shivered, even in the May sun, remembering the winter that her grandfather had died, the long weeks of illness and hushed voices in the cabin. Now she chose to remember Granfer's lilting voice as he told of the cleverness of Cornish smugglers against English revenuers, or strange adventures of fishing boats out at sea.

Beside Granfer's stone were three smaller ones. One was marked: *Infant daughter of John & Lavinia Mather, b. & d. 1841.* The other two were for each of the stillborn sons. Florence had been two years old, then three, then four, when her unknown sister and brothers had been born.

Gran knelt to place her hand over the grass in front of Granfer's stone. Florence knelt and did the same while Gran murmured a few Cornish words.

At each of the small graves they knelt, and then Florence stood up and helped Gran to rise. Arm in arm they walked back toward the wagon. The scent of decaying lilacs wafted from the bushes along the chapel wall.

Chapter 5

At the Smithy

One morning in June as Katie brought in the milk, Pa said, "We'll wash the sheep after the Sabbath and shear next week, if the weather holds."

"One of the shears is cracked," said Will. "I'd best ride over to the smithy this afternoon."

"Take the other shears as well," said Pa. "A dull blade makes twice the work."

"Pa," said Katie, "might I go along with Will?"

"*I'd* be of more use," said Amos. "Owen lets me turn the whetstone."

"*I'll* go," said Thomas. "I can help. I heard that Big Jim Doane is bringing the chestnut to be shod."

Pa smiled. "Once you've finished your chores, you may all go." He glanced at Matilda. "Have you no reason to visit the smithy today?"

Matilda did not look up from the oatmeal she was stirring. "I'd best stay home and help Ma with the sewing. Only a fortnight till Will's wedding."

Katie and her brothers mucked out the sheep pens and cleared burdock weeds from the pasture. At mid-morning, Katie climbed into the back of the wagon with Amos. Thomas drove, and Will sat beside him. As they pulled onto the wooden road, Katie listened to the rhythmic clopping of the horses' hooves on the planks and the rolling of the wagon wheels.

"Just look at how well my orchard is coming along," Will said as they passed his new house. "I've a mind to exhibit those apples at the county fair."

Soon the wagon turned off the plank road and headed up the section-line road, climbing slowly over the hill they all knew as The Rise. The highest spot in the whole county, it gave a splendid view of the countryside. Katie knew that in a fortnight the Cornish settlers would build their Midsummer fire on this high ground.

When they pulled up in the Caswell smithyard, Katie and Amos hopped out almost before the wheels stopped turning. Katie saw Si and Daniel Doane at the watering trough.

"Katie!" they called. "Come see our boats!"

Katie walked over to admire the fleet of oak-leaf ships sailing in the still waters.

"Grandpa said we're not to go inside the smithy," said Daniel. "Lightning's a spirited horse."

Katie glanced through the open doors of the smithy. Amos was already perched on the far side of the forge. Between Big Jim and Charlie Doane, the chestnut stallion pawed and whinnied, shying from the heat of the forge and the pounding of the iron. Holding him steady with their strong arms, the two Doane men had faces red enough to match Owen's. Katie turned away and studied the broadsides posted on the smithy door. A new sign announced Independence Day doings in Rochester.

"Hold tight!" called Big Jim, as Lightning snorted and tried to break free.

Katie grabbed hold of the Doane boys, who had darted toward the smithy door at the sound of their grandpa's shout.

Thomas gave a low, calming whistle. He stepped forward slowly, directly in front of the excited animal. "Easy now, boy." He stood without moving, looking the horse straight in the eyes, and then he held out the flat of his palm. Katie could see the great nostrils flare as Lightning sniffed the outstretched hand. Then Thomas stroked the stallion's neck and took hold of the halter. Without a word Charlie moved aside to give him room.

Thomas rubbed the white streak on the stallion's muzzle. "Have no fear, my friend. Owen will have you fitted in no time."

Big Jim shook his head and smiled. As Thomas settled down the horse, Owen stepped along the animal's side, one hand moving steadily over the chestnut coat and down the hindquarters. Carefully Owen lifted Lightning's hind foot and held a lightweight racing shoe against the hoof. He eyed the fit, then set down the hoof. Stepping over to the forge, he took up the tongs and placed the horseshoe into the fire.

"Amos, work the bellows, will 'ee?" Owen asked in a low voice.

"Yes, sir." Amos grabbed the handles and pumped them together so that each gust of air caused the fire to burn hotter.

Owen took the glowing red horseshoe out of the fire and held it to the end of his anvil as he swiftly hammered it into shape. A moment later the horseshoe hit the bucket of water with a steaming hiss. While the blacksmith nailed the racing shoe into place, Thomas kept up his soothing talk to Lightning. It occurred to Katie that Thomas generally had more to say to horses than to humans.

Katie still held the hands of Si and Daniel. "Don't that hurt the horse?" Silas asked, watching Owen pound a nail through Lightning's hoof, then deftly bend the point.

"No, the hoof is like a fingernail," Katie said. Still, her own toes curled up inside her shoes as she said it.

Daniel pointed to a sign near the Independence Day broadside. "*READ and PONDER*. What does that mean, Katie?"

"*Ponder* means to think about," said Katie. "It says, *Read and ponder the Fugitive Slave Law which disregards all the ordinary securities of personal liberty, which tramples on the Constitution–*"

Daniel tugged at Katie's dress. "What does that mean?"

"It . . . it means we should think about slaves and the slavery laws. About whether people ought to be allowed to have slaves. And whether people ought to help slaves to escape."

Big Jim walked out of the smithy and lifted his grandson into his arms. "We don't need to think about slaves, Dan'l. Down South the folks need slaves to work the plantations. That's all." He handed Daniel and Si up to Charlie, who had mounted his black horse.

Big Jim mounted the newly shod chestnut, grunting as he swung into the saddle. Just before he rode out of the yard, he spat on the ground, and Katie heard him say to Charlie, "Abolitionist or no, Caswell is the best smith around."

Owen stepped out of the smithy and looked around the yard. "So all the McEachrons but Matilda have come to see me."

"She's finishing her dress for the wedding," Katie said.

"Midsummer is a fine time to marry," said Owen. "Gives a farmer a run of days to settle in."

Will said, "If you'd mend these shears, I reckon we'll finish our shearing well before then."

When Katie came home from school one afternoon the next week, Father and Thomas were each shearing a ewe outside the barn. Amos held an unshorn lamb, waiting for one of the shearers to finish. Will was bundling fleeces. "Put on a work dress, Katie," Pa said, "and tell your mother we'll keep on till full dark."

Katie flung her books and slate onto the kitchen table and hurried upstairs. A few minutes later she was standing alongside Will, digging her fingers deep into the new-shorn fleece.

"We're to bundle the wool, not tear it apart," warned Will.

"I know, but it's so soft I can't help myself."

Will spread the fleece on a piece of canvas and used the shears to clip away the matted dirt on the edges. Then Katie folded the fleece so that the thickest wool lay on top. She picked up the bundled fleece and pushed it deep into the long woolsack with the others.

The farmyard was deep in shadows when the McEachrons stopped shearing for the night. Pa and Will and Thomas walked stiffly toward the house. Tonight there would be no gathering on the porch after the evening meal. Katie knew Pa and the boys would be in bed even before she and Ma and Matilda finished the dishes. Harvest days were like that, too, as was planting time.

Still, Katie had a question that could not wait. "Pa, when will you take the wool to Haymarket Square?"

"Not before it's off the sheep."

The boys chuckled.

Katie ignored them. "Might I go along when you take the wool to Racine? Last year you took Amos. And you said that I might go this summer. I reckon Miss Waite won't mind if I miss a day of school."

Pa raised his eyebrows.

"I mean to say," Katie said hastily, "that going to market would be . . . a fine way of learning. I could figure the weight and the price per pound and all."

"Everyone's taking wool to market now," Pa said. "We'll bide our time. By next month when school's out, we'll get a better price."

He smiled. "Yes, Katherine, you will have your journey to Haymarket Square."

June 8, 1852

It is shearing time. Amos was able to miss two days of school to stay home and help, first to wash the sheep and then to shear. I wanted to stay and help wash, but Pa said that Amos would be help enough.

When I protested, Thomas said that I'd be more hindrance than help.

I had to bite my tongue to keep silence, but Pa scolded Thomas for such talk.

I did help with bundling after school today. And Pa has promised that I will be the one to travel to Racine with him when it's time to take the wool to market.

Chapter 6

Midsummer Eve

Florence had already washed up the breakfast dishes when she heard Katie's rap at the kitchen door and heard her call, "Aren't you ready for school?"

Florence shook her head. "Mother needs me to make ready for the wedding dance tomorrow."

Katie's face fell. "Why, this isn't even *your* family's wedding." Her face brightened. "Florence, you go on to school and I'll help your ma."

Mrs. Mather swept into the kitchen, her arms full of bedding. "That 'ee will not, Katherine McEachron. Now be off. Florence has no time for idle chatter." She continued out the door into the yard.

Katie sighed. "Yesterday I asked Miss Waite why we call the first day of summer 'Midsummer.' She had no answer, except to say that it is the longest day of the year, and the Midsummer fire was a heathen practice. She said pagans used to dance around such fires and offer sacrifices."

"What did 'ee say to that?" asked Florence, troubled to think of her schoolteacher objecting to this custom.

"I told her my brother Will was going to the fire and did she think he was a heathen?"

Mrs. Mather appeared in the doorway with the long laundry paddle in her hand. Katie grabbed her dinner pail and disappeared out the door.

"Longest day of the year or no," said Mrs. Mather, "I never have daylight enough. Next year I may keep 'ee home from school all summer to help."

Florence spent much of the morning frying up cinnamon twists and listening to her mother fret. She hoped that the talk of missing school next summer was just an idle threat. As she twisted dough and dropped the twists into hot oil, she wondered what her previous schoolteacher Will McEachron would think of the Cornish celebration that evening, now that he was engaged to marry Grace Caswell.

At last she dared to ask, "Mother, may I go and collect the herbs now, before the sun is high?"

Mrs. Mather frowned but handed her a basket. "Be back in time to set the table for the noon meal."

Florence took the basket to Gran's garden. There she found St. John's wort, with its star-shaped yellow flowers, and purple spikes of vervain. The scent of rosemary and thyme filled the air as she plucked the herbs. At the edge of the hayfield, she picked stems of purple clover and carefully cut a stinging-nettle. From the McEachrons' field across the section-line road, she took a few stalks of ripening wheat and a strand of bindweed.

Near Gran's cabin Florence broke a cluster of leaves from the oldest oak. She paused, savoring the solitude, to speak a bit of a poem by Ralph Waldo Emerson that she knew by heart:

> *The word by seers or sibyls told,*
> *In groves of oak or fanes of gold,*
> *Still floats upon the morning wind,*
> *Still whispers to the willing mind.*

Between the midday washing-up and tea-time, Florence cleaned upstairs. First she smoothed the quilts and wiped the windowsills in the bedrooms. Later she worked in the ballroom. She removed old candle stubs from the sconces that lined the walls and used a rag soaked in vinegar to polish the tin reflectors. Then she washed the long windows and swept and scrubbed the vast floor.

Left to her own thoughts, beyond her mother's grumbling or the comings and goings of teamsters, Florence started to imagine ways to decorate the inn for the coming wedding. She had some wonderful ideas for the spool of white ribbon from the Ives Grove store.

When she came down to the kitchen, she found Grace's father laying a great sack on the table. "Look inside, Florence, will 'ee?"

Florence reached into the mouth of the sack and pulled out a fruit of vivid yellow.

She held the fruit to her face and breathed its citrus scent, wondering in what far-off place a hand had plucked it from a tree.

"We'll have real lemonade on my Grace's wedding day," Mr. Caswell said. "Ordered them special, I did."

Even Mrs. Mather was pleased at the prospect. "For years we've made do with sumac," she said. "We'll have a rare treat indeed."

"Is there anything else I can bring 'ee, Vin?" Mr. Caswell asked. "Will 'ee have me send my wife over to help?"

"What nonsense!" said Mrs. Mather. "Florence and I can manage. Be off now."

Mr. Caswell lingered in the doorway. "We're grateful for all 'ee do." He nodded to Florence. "Mind 'ee don't work past the lighting of the fire."

As the sun was sinking behind the roof of the log barn, Mr. Mather brought the wagon up to the inn's watering trough. He called a farewell to Mrs. Mather and helped Gran and Florence into the wagon.

When the wagon was still some distance away from The Rise, Florence could see glowing torches. Soon she could make out the figures standing in clusters on the hill. She recognized Owen Caswell by his sturdy build.

When the wagon reached the top of The Rise, Owen stepped over and held out his strong arms to her. Florence put both her hands in his and jumped to the ground. Owen's firm grip brought back vivid memories of Midsummers past. Well she remembered taking hands with Owen on one side, Grace on the other, as a long chain of young folks ran laughing and leaping over the dying embers.

The Moyles and Vyvyans and Shephards had already arrived. Amanda Shephard balanced her baby brother on one hip, grasped the hand of a toddler, and listened to a little girl tugging at her skirt. Florence thought of all the work Amanda had to do since her mother died. Just last summer Amanda's mother, great with child, had stood with them at the Midsummer fire.

Grace Caswell stepped out from the shadows. In the torch-light her eyes gleamed and her dark curls were wreathed in wild roses. She turned and laughed softly into the darkness. Almost shyly Will McEachron stepped into the circle of light.

"We welcome 'ee, William," said Old Man Caswell.

Silently the other settlers formed a circle around the brush pile. "Friends," said Old Man Caswell, "the sun has traveled its long dance across the sky. We gather together once more to remember those we have lost . . ." he nodded to the Shephards, ". . . and those we have welcomed in the year past.

"'Tis a blessing," he continued, "to be amongst countrymen who have traveled the road from the far shores of Cornwall to this good land. May all who travel life's difficult and dangerous roads reach safe haven as well."

Florence set his words in her mind.

Gran stepped closer to the woodpile and murmured in Cornish. Old Man Caswell leaned in to touch his torch to the twigs and dry leaves. Tiny flames licked at the kindling, and a glow crept from branch to branch. Gran held the bunch of herbs high over the fire and chanted:

> *Thousandfold let good seed spring,*
> *Wicked weeds fast withering*
> *Let this fire kill.*

She tossed the herbs into the flames, which hissed and steamed.

Florence looked at the circle of faces, old and young and every age between. The younger ones were caught up in the moment, afire with excitement over the power of heat and light. She saw Grace whisper to Will and knew that the two would take hands to leap over the embers when the fire died low.

The oldest among the settlers–Gran Mather, the elder Caswells, and Granfer Shephard–wore pensive faces. Gran had told Florence that on Midsummer Eve in Cornwall one could see a chain of fires on the cliff tops stretching all along the sea-coast. What must it be like to know that one would never again see those fires or take hands with old friends and kinfolk?

Here in this circle, Florence was proud to be linked by blood and custom to the land she knew only through stories and songs, the land where others shared in the keeping of the fires.

Chapter 7

Wedding Day

After the noon meal on Midsummer Day, Katie and Matilda went upstairs to change into their new dresses for the wedding. Katie slipped the deep-crimson calico dress over her head and was thrilled to find that Ma had hemmed the skirt longer than schoolgirl length. "Button me up, Matilda," she said, turning her back to her sister.

As Matilda buttoned the dress, Katie admired the shiny black buttons and braid that adorned the dress. "Isn't it beautiful?" she asked, twisting around. "When are you going to get your dress on?"

"Perhaps if you'd hold still long enough, I'd have time to dress." Matilda patted Katie's back and handed her a hairbrush.

Katie sat down on the bed, undid her braids, and began brushing her hair. "Your hair is ever so much prettier than mine," she said. "Mine's just middlin' brown, but yours glimmers like brocade." Katie studied her sister's shining auburn hair against the sky-blue calico of her dress. With her pale complexion and green eyes, Matilda looked as beautiful as an illustration in a book of tales.

"Your hair will darken as you get older," Matilda said. "And if you'd remember to wear your sunbonnet, you'd have fair skin as well. Come button me."

When the girls came downstairs, they found the family out-side. Amos sat on the porch rail. In the yard Thomas stood alongside Rowena, whose harness fittings sparkled in the sun-light. The buggy was scrubbed and polished down to the very spokes. Katie looked at Will, standing stiffly on the porch in his new black suit.

"Aren't you happy to be getting married, Will? You don't look well," Katie spun around to make her crimson skirt twirl. "Ever since planting, all you've talked about is 'Grace this' and 'Grace that.' And now your wedding is here, and you don't seem excited at all."

"Oh, leave him alone," said Thomas. "He'll be listening to a woman every day for the rest of his life."

"Wagons coming!" said Amos.

"Good that you swung open the tollgate earlier. Who'll mind the gate while we're at the church?" Katie asked. She skipped off the porch to get a better look at the two wagons. The first was driven by Grace's father, with her mother beside him. From the seat in back Grace nodded to the McEachrons.

"Oh, Will, isn't she beautiful?" cried Katie. "She's got flow-ers in her hair!"

Owen Caswell was driving the second wagon, with Gran Caswell beside him. Katie waved to Grace's brother and sister, Caleb and Emma, who sat in the back with Old Man Caswell.

Pa stepped onto the porch and rested his hand on Will's shoulder. "Time to go, son." Ma, Matilda, and Katie climbed into the back seat of the buggy. Pa and Will sat together up front, their broad shoulders touching. Thomas handed the reins to Pa, then hopped onto the back of the buggy with Amos.

When they passed the Mather Inn, Katie saw Thomas slide off the back of the buggy, then run toward the inn yard, arms churning, a comical sight in his Sunday best. She opened her mouth to ask where he was going, but Matilda shushed her. Katie looked at Ma, who nodded mysteriously at Will's back. "He'll join us soon" was all she said.

At the edge of the Doane property, the buggy turned north, to where the Scotch Settlement church stood on its lone acre. The Reverend Macgraw was standing outside the white clapboard church.

The Caswells were already inside, except for Owen, who helped Matilda from the buggy, holding her hand in both of his.

"Nothing brings out beauty like a wedding day," said Owen.

Then he turned to Will. "Well, my friend, are 'ee ready?"

Outside the church Ma adjusted Katie's hat and straightened Amos' collar, then took Pa's arm and stepped through the door. Katie followed them to a front pew. Mrs. Macgraw was pumping away at the organ. Katie turned around in her seat to see Grace standing in the back corner of the church. Sunlight shone on her cream-colored dress and on the blossoms in her dark hair.

Will and Owen walked down the aisle with the Reverend Macgraw and took their places alongside the Bible stand. Behind them came Thomas, grinning as he slid into the family pew. "What were you doing at the inn?" Katie whispered. Thomas just smirked, then made his face very solemn.

Grace walked up the aisle, her shining eyes fixed on Will, who stepped forward to meet her. Matilda and Owen took their places on either side of the bride and groom.

Katie bowed her head for the prayer, but she was burning with curiosity. As she shared a hymn book with Thomas, she asked him again where he had gone. He merely winked and sang louder:

Let not the world's deceitful cares
The rising plant destroy,
But let it yield a hundred fold
The fruits of peace and joy.

After the brief service, Katie saw Thomas slip out the church door. She had no chance to follow him, for Ma pushed her toward the bride and groom. Will's embrace knocked Katie's hat sideways. Grace said, "Now I have a new little sister" as she kissed Katie's cheek. Katie wriggled away and hurried out to find Thomas.

There he stood at the church steps, holding the reins of a beautiful white horse hitched to a brand-new wagon. The wagon was painted blue and decorated with white scrollwork.

Behind Katie, Amos said proudly, "The mare is Pa and Ma's gift to Will and Grace. Thomas and Big Jim bought her last week. Isn't she a beauty?"

"Why didn't I know about it?"

"Back in May," Amos went on, "Grace's folks bought the wagon at the carriage factory in Rochester. Kept it hidden at the inn all this time."

Katie looked from one smiling brother to the other. "Why didn't anybody tell me?"

"Aw, Katie," said Thomas. "You know you can never keep your mouth shut."

Pa escorted the bride and groom outside. "Time to take your own reins, son," he said.

Right behind him came Mr. Caswell.

"Oh, Father!" Grace said. She seemed about to cry.

Mr. Caswell stepped forward, past Will, to help Grace into the wagon. "Up 'ee go, missy," he said. Grace smiled mistily and bent to give her father a kiss.

Thomas offered advice as if the bride and groom had never seen a horse before. "She's plenty gentle, Grace," Thomas said. "Her name's Sunshine," he added, and at last he handed the reins to Will.

Katie folded her arms and glared out at the horse and wagon. "It's not fair! Why didn't anybody tell me?" Then she caught sight of her father's face and broke off. "I'm sorry, Pa."

"I'm sorry you're troubled, Daughter. No one meant you harm in keeping the secret."

"Load up for the wedding dinner!" Owen called. He took Matilda's hand and led her to his wagon. Emma and Caleb hurried to scramble up into the back of Owen's wagon. Thomas brought the McEachron buggy round to the church steps. "I'll drive, Pa," he offered.

"Not today, son." Pa turned to Katie. "Daughter, would you take us to the Caswell dinner?"

Katie lifted her chin and smiled. "Yes, sir, I will."

She couldn't help but toss a smug look toward Thomas, who said to Amos, "Reckon we'd best find another ride." The two trotted off toward the Caswell wagons.

Eagerly Katie took the reins up front, while Pa helped Ma into the back seat before taking his place beside Katie. Katie gave Rowena a slap with the reins and was almost jerked off the seat as the mare pulled them out of the churchyard, following the bridal couple and the two Caswell wagons. When they reached the plank road, Katie drove alongside the planks until she came to an extended board, where she guided the front wheel up onto the planks. The buggy lurched up, not as smoothly as when her father drove.

As they approached the inn, Katie called, "Florence, look at me!" lifting the reins high into the air.

"Don't confuse the horse," said Pa, bringing her hands down. "Give her firm but gentle guidance."

A teamster was watering his horses. "Look, Matilda!" Katie called to the wagon up ahead. "'It's Mister Banvard!"

"Hush, Katie," said Ma. "You oughtn't to shout."

In the wagon ahead, Matilda turned to look toward the inn, then quickly turned away. Mr. Banvard raised his hat to her in a friendly salute. The procession continued without pause through the open tollgate, as those going to and from a place of worship did not need to pay toll.

"Stop here," Pa told Katie as they passed the gate. "I'll swing the gate shut. John Mather said he'd keep watch while we're at dinner."

Katie could hardly wait for Pa to help her out of the buggy when they pulled up to the Mather Inn that evening. Mrs. Mather, wearing a lace-trimmed apron over her Sunday dress, greeted them. "I've never come in the front door before," said Katie, stepping into the front hall. A big white bow adorned the newel post of the staircase, and the banister had been wrapped with white ribbon all the way to the second floor.

"Did Florence do that?" Katie asked, nodding toward the banister. "Where is she?"

"Florence is in the ballroom," Mrs. Mather said. "Go on up."

Katie sailed grandly up the front stairs. She stepped through an arched doorway framed with white bunting and garlands of ivy into the ballroom. Florence was standing on a chair placing the last fresh candle into a sconce. White ribbons adorned each of the twelve sconces along the walls, and the entire room was scented with roses. On the far wall hung the Bride's Album quilt. The squares featuring the inn and the schoolhouse made the quilt look like a great map of Yorkville.

"Oh, Florence," said Katie, "I can hardly believe how beautiful this is." She lifted her skirts and curtseyed deeply, then danced across the shining floor.

Florence said, "I expect every garden in Yorkville has made a contribution." She joined Katie in the alcove overlooking the front door.

Katie leaned out the open window. "Here come the Caswells!" she cried, "and the Shephards close behind."

"Katie, don't hang out the window," came Matilda's voice from the hallway. She turned to Florence. "The ballroom looks splendid. You must have been hours at this."

Florence smiled. "Mother thought I spent too much time, until Mister Banvard said the ballroom looked as fine as any he'd *ever* seen."

"I saw him this afternoon as we passed," Matilda said. "Did he stay long?"

"He said he remembered Mother's cooking with such pleasure he'd like to take another meal at the Mather Inn," Florence said. "And he asked me to send his kind regards to the McEachrons."

"Did he say anything else?"

Katie turned to look at her sister. "What else should he have said?"

Matilda shrugged. "Nothing," she said. "Nothing at all."

Soon it seemed to Katie that everybody she knew was upstairs or downstairs or out on the porch or in the yard. From old Granfer Shephard, who must be nearly eighty, to the newest Waite baby, all the settlers of Yorkville had come to join in the celebration. In the ballroom the fiddles of Mr. Shephard and Old Man Caswell sang out into the summer evening. Young and old paired off to join in the country dances.

Katie was surprised to see Will standing before her. "May I have this dance?" he said.

"Oughtn't you to ask Grace?"

Will grinned. "She's promised me every waltz."

He and Katie joined the other guests of all ages forming two lines down the hall. With great energy they romped through the figures of the dance. Will swung Katie so hard her skirts spun like a top, and she was nearly breathless when the music stopped. Then Will bowed, she curtseyed, and each went off to find a new partner.

Katie danced the next reel with Caleb. The third was an unfamiliar dance for which Old Man Caswell called the figures. With Pa as her partner, Katie learned the steps easily. "You're a quick study, Daughter," he said, and Katie beamed.

Later Katie followed Florence up and down the back stairs as her friend carried trays of refreshments to the older guests and made sure the musicians' water pitcher was always full. When the setting sun bathed the ballroom in golden light, Old Man Caswell signaled Will and Grace to stand beside him. "Now, I'm not a man of many words," he began.

The settlers chuckled.

"But I've a few to share with 'ee tonight," he continued with a smile. "My own granddaughter's been wed this day, and I thank 'ee for sharing the joy of the occasion. Wherever we began our lives, out east or over the sea, we've made our homes in Wisconsin. 'Tis a blessing to live in a place where neighbor helps neighbor. When one family mourns, we all mourn, and when one rejoices, we all rejoice! If it please the Maker, may we all dwell together," he paused for dramatic effect, "with Grace . . . and good Will."

Laughter rippled over the room, and then the voices echoed, "To Grace and good Will!"

Mr. Shephard called out, "Owen, favor us with a song, will 'ee?"

Others took up the cry, "Aye, a song from Owen Caswell."

Owen smiled. "What would 'ee have me sing?"

"Give us 'The Jolly Wagoner!'" said Old Man Caswell, as he raised his fiddle to his chin.

> *When first I went a-wagoning,*
> *A-wagoning did go,*
> *I filled my parents' hearts*
> *Full of sorrow, grief and woe.*

Here Owen cocked his head at his grandfather, whose bow scraped the strings with a comic discord.

> *And many are the hardships*
> *That I have since gone through.*

Owen held the last note and came down hard on the refrain:

> *And sing WHOA, my lads, sing WHOA!*
> *Drive on, my lads, I-HO!*
> *And who wouldn't lead the life*
> *Of a jolly wagoner?*

Still singing, Owen stepped over to Florence, who was standing with a tray of lemonade in her hand.

> *For 'tis a cold and stormy night*
> *And I'm wet to the skin,*
> *I will bear it with contentment*
> *Till I get me to the inn—*

Deftly he hoisted a tin mug and winked at her.

> *And then I'll get a-drinking*
> *With the landlord and his kin!*

Florence blushed, the crowd roared, and everyone joined in on the final refrain.

Owen bowed, and Old Man Caswell signaled for another dance. Katie tapped her foot to the music and saw the Cornish settlers smile in recognition and look about for partners. Mr. Mather led Florence out to the floor. Shepherds and Caswells, Vyvyans and Moyles hurried out to form sets.

None of the Yankee settlers seemed to know the dance, so Katie wandered down the front stairs and peeked into the parlor. Gran Mather sat amid the bounty of wedding gifts. There were skeins of wool and jars of preserves, covered baskets and bright new tins, a sack of sugar, a pair of dish towels tied up in red ribbon, and a wreath of kitchen herbs. Opal Doane was sitting beside Laura Waite, who was nursing her baby. Gran Caswell and Mrs. Doane were listening to the Widow Everett describe her latest malady. On the parlor rug two babies were playing while their mothers danced upstairs.

Katie retreated from the parlor. In the dining room, she stopped to nibble a Cornish saffron cake, plump with currants and raisins and smelling of cinnamon and nutmeg. The table had been draped with a white cloth, and a porcelain vase of roses and larkspur stood among the bowls of strawberries and platters of cinnamon twists.

Katie heard the deep voices of men outside on the porch. Big Jim Doane was talking about Will's white mare. Charlie Doane was passing a jug of something to Jasper Everett.

Katie wondered why none of the Doanes had been upstairs dancing. At the schoolhouse dances Charlie never rested till he had given every girl a turn.

June 24, 1852

Grace and Good Will's wedding dance was wonderful. I danced till late in the night, when my feet and legs were aching.

But the whole of the evening, I never once danced with any of the Doanes. They weren't in the ballroom.

Florence slaved for days to get the inn ready. Perhaps I oughtn't to use that word. But she worked very hard to make the Mather Inn beautiful. I looked around the room and saw all the womenfolk who had made squares for Grace's quilt. It seems that we have threads holding us all together.

I wonder, though, what holds the menfolk together.

Chapter 8

Strawberry Jam

O n a humid morning at the end of June, Florence reveled in unaccustomed freedom as she and Katie made their way through the underbrush along the creek that ran along the back of the McEachron fields. They carried baskets for berrying. At Katie's suggestion, they had tied bright kerchiefs over their hair instead of wearing sunbonnets.

After breakfast, Mrs. Mather and Gran had left for the tin and copper shop in Rochester. As the wagon exited the yard, Mr. Mather had turned to Florence. "Well now," he said. "No teamster needs a hot dinner on such a day. I'll serve up cold pasties to any who stop. Enjoy a holiday till tea-time, will 'ee?"

Florence had spent part of her morning reading one of Emerson's essays. When she read the lines:

Books are for the scholar's idle times.
When he can read God directly, the hour is too precious
to be wasted in other men's transcripts of their readings.

she took it as a sign. In a flash, she closed the volume and hurried across the pasture to find Katie.

Now, as they reached the banks of the creek, Katie leaped onto a half-submerged rock. With a grin at Florence, she held her basket in her arms like a baby.

"I'm Eliza!" she cried, "and I must cross the river before the slave catchers come!" She put one hand up to her cheek in mock terror. "Lawd have mercy, the bloodhounds!" As Florence watched from the bank, Katie leaped from rock to rock, cradling her basket and shrieking.

"Oh, Katie!" Florence said. "One oughtn't make a game of slavery! What would Harriet Beecher Stowe think?"

Katie smiled. "She'd be happy I'd read *Uncle Tom's Cabin.*" Suddenly her foot slipped.

"Mercy, ain't the Ohio River cold!" she said in her Eliza voice, as she scrambled up the other bank.

Up ahead, Florence pulled aside the trailing grapevines that covered the entrance to a shady bower. "Remember when we were little and made plans to run away and live in here? We were going to live on strawberries and grapes."

Katie had already pushed on to the secret place they called Strawberry Glen. "Look," she called, "there's more red than green!"

Florence joined her in the sunlit clearing. Katie was right. Lush red fruits and white blossoms shone brightly against the green leaves. Florence knelt to pull a few berries from the stem, marveling at their warmth in her hand.

Katie talked steadily as she picked. "Grace adored her wedding quilt," she said. "She told me the lilac square was her favorite because Will brought lilacs when he first came calling." She gazed over the strawberry patch.

"Wouldn't Strawberry Glen make a beautiful quilt square?" Katie sat back on her heels. "Crimson berries . . . and the jagged edges of green leaves."

"Have 'ee scraps of that crimson calico?"

"Florence! You and I could make a Strawberry Patch quilt!"

Florence shook her head. "I'd not have time for such an undertaking with all the preserving to do."

"Florence! Let's make strawberry preserves today. Just cook down the berries, throw in some sugar, and fill the jars."

"Katie McEachron! There's more to preserving than 'throwing in some sugar.' I've spent more hours in the kitchen than 'ee."

"Wouldn't our mothers be pleased to find the work all done?"

Florence pictured her mother's face upon seeing neat rows of ruby-red jars. "Well," she said, "'ee may be right at that."

By noon, it was hotter than ever, but on the way back from the creek, Florence stopped to fill her apron with tiny green apples to thicken the jam. By the time the girls set their baskets on the porch of Gran's cabin, their dresses were wet with sweat.

"Why don't we work in the inn instead?" Katie asked. "It's so much nicer."

"Gran won't mind our making a mess," Florence said. She did not add that her mother might. "We first have to boil the jars." She scurried over to the inn to get a crate of empty glass jars from the pantry. She and Katie hauled buckets of water, enough to rinse the jars and fill the canning kettle.

Katie wiped her brow. "Hot day to be starting fires."

"We can sit on the porch," said Florence. Katie sat on the bench outside the little cabin while Florence went inside.

Here, in Gran's cabin, Florence always felt at ease. The bowls and platters on the shelves were arranged in a casual but natural order.

She stirred the embers inside the stove and added a handful of kindling. She consulted Gran's recipe book, a small leather-bound volume filled with pages of spidery writing and bulging with extra scraps of paper. Then she stepped outside to the porch with a kettle, a bowl, and a paring knife.

While Katie pared the apples, Florence sat on the steps and deftly hulled the strawberries, dropping the fruit into the kettle and tossing the green stems into the herb garden next to the porch.

"Ma always chases me out of the kitchen when it's preserving time," Katie confessed. "She says I'm more hindrance than help."

"I'm sure she'll say otherwise after today." Florence dropped the last of her berries into the kettle.

She and Katie went into the cabin, where Florence set the kettle on the hot stove top. "Dump the apple slices into the kettle," she said, "then get me six cups of sugar."

"Six cups? That sounds like far too much."

Florence stared at Katie. "'Tisn't I who has been chased out of the kitchen for thirteen years!"

"You needn't get so high and mighty, Florence Mather. All I did was ask a simple question." Sulkily Katie scooped the sugar from a barrel and carried the bowl back to the stove.

Florence carefully poured the sugar into the kettle and began to stir. Katie took the empty bowl out onto the porch, and when Florence glanced out the window, she could see her friend busily licking sugar-sticky fingers.

The wood fire had warmed the cabin thoroughly, and Florence's face was damp with heat. Intent on her stirring, she called out to Katie, "Prop open the door."

"You needn't order me about," said Katie, not leaving her seat.

"Then come and stir while I do it!"

With a sigh Katie entered the room and took the big wooden spoon.

Florence frowned, wishing that Katie might have thought to prop open the door on her way inside. "Keep steadily at the stirring," Florence instructed. "We mustn't let the sugar burn."

"It's awfully hot in here," said Katie after a while, laying the spoon against the side of the kettle and pulling off her kerchief.

"Katie! Don't stop stirring!"

Katie rolled her eyes and picked up the spoon. "We should have made shortcake instead."

"'Twasn't my idea to spend the day in the kitchen," Florence snapped. She peered into the thickening mixture in the kettle. "And now look what 'ee've done. There's a hair in the jam!"

"You sound as bossy as your mother."

Florence was outraged. She reached to take the spoon from Katie, who held it more tightly and stirred with such fury that a bit of boiling sauce splashed onto Florence.

Florence yelped and clutched her forearm. "Look what 'ee've done!" she said. "Here I do the work of a grown woman every day, and all 'ee do is go to school and play about like a child! Katie McEachron, 'ee don't know nails from oats!"

She and Katie glared at each other across the steaming kettle.

Katie stopped stirring and strode toward the door. "I am not a child. I'll take my berries home for shortcake. As you're such a fine worker, you can keep all that jam to yourself!" She flounced out of the cabin.

Tears dripping down her face, Florence had no choice but to continue to stir the bubbling mixture. The burn on her arm throbbed, but she could never allow six cups of sugar to be wasted.

She heard her father's whistle in the yard and then his familiar step on the porch.

The door creaked open.

"A strange sort of holiday this is," Mr. Mather said with a smile. Then he saw her face.

"Tell me what's troubling 'ee."

Still stirring, Florence spilled out the story.

"It seems we've a task at hand to finish," said Mr. Mather, stepping up to the kettle. "What would 'ee have me do?"

Chapter 9

An Unexpected Guest

Late that evening, Florence sat with her family in the kitchen of the inn. A row of ruby-red jars lined the long wooden counter. Gran had been quick to praise Florence's efforts.

When Mrs. Mather had closely examined, then pronounced the preserves satisfactory, Florence and her father exchanged a smile of relief.

Now the Mathers sipped their tea and listened to the rumble of thunder overhead. Florence's burnt forearm still ached when she raised the cup. The wind picked up, and from the barn across the yard came a nervous whickering as the horses felt the approach of the storm.

At last the rain came, lashing against the windowpanes.

"A good dousing's what we need," said Mr. Mather.

Mrs. Mather said, "Did 'ee close the windows upstairs, Florence?"

"'Tis glad I am to be snug here and not about on such a night," said Gran.

Again in silence, they listened to the wind and the rain.

As the storm paused for a moment, Mr. Mather stopped with his cup halfway to his lips and tilted his head. Then came two quick raps on the kitchen door.

Florence saw her father look across at Gran.

Mrs. Mather set down her cup. "Who'd come to the back door at this hour?" she said, already on her feet and straightening her apron as she crossed the room.

"Why, Mister Banvard," she said, "what brings 'ee here so late? Do come in. Mind 'ee wipe those boots."

At once Mr. Mather was beside his wife at the door. The teamster was drenched, black hair pasted to his face as he stepped inside, looked cautiously about the kitchen, then glanced into the dining room.

He looked intently at Mr. Mather. "I've a large parcel," he said, "which I cannot deliver."

Florence saw her father's face grow sober. The teamster continued, "I'm sorry to trouble you so late . . ." now he was looking across the room at Gran, ". . . but I knew nowhere else to turn."

Mrs. Mather stared from the visitor to Mr. Mather to Gran. "Are 'ee all mad?" she said. "Put that wagon in the barn and come in out of the wet. Surely this parcel will wait till the morn."

Abruptly Mr. Mather reached for his barn coat on the peg beside the door. "I'll give 'ee a hand with the horses," he said, and the two men plunged out into the rain.

Mrs. Mather shook her head and sighed. "Florence, see to the little room off the stairs."

"Lavinia," said Gran, "We'll have one more guest tonight."

"Yes, Banvard is unexpected. I can't think why he'd travel so late."

"Lavinia." So softly that Florence could hardly hear, Gran said, "Banvard has with him a dark stranger who must not be found."

"Not be found? Are 'ee telling riddles?"

Then Mr. Mather was at the door, his arm around a figure

whose head and shoulders were covered with a woolen blanket. Behind them came Banvard, who pulled a chair closer to the wood stove. Mr. Mather eased the newcomer onto the chair, where the wrapped-up fellow slumped forward, almost falling.

"Build up the fire, Vin," Mr. Mather said sharply. "This man is ill and wet through."

Immediately Mrs. Mather stepped over to the wood box for kindling.

Gran knelt before the sick man and spoke so low that Florence could not hear. Behind her, Banvard looked on. "Jonah has been feverish since I picked him up."

Florence stared at the blanket-shrouded figure.

Mrs. Mather blew upon the fire and closed the little iron door. She came to stand behind Gran. When Mrs. Mather bent to peer under the blanket, she gasped. "Why, this man is . . . he's a . . ." her voice failed her a moment, then came out in a whisper. "He's a fugitive."

She turned to Mr. Mather. "A fugitive, John. We can't have him here."

Gran said, "We do have him here, and we'd best get him to bed."

Mrs. Mather crossed her arms. "I'll not put this family at risk! A thousand dollar fine, John! A prison sentence. We'd lose everything–our stock in the plank road, even the inn."

Mr. Mather said gently, "I should have spoken with 'ee sooner, Vin, but I did not want to trouble 'ee. 'Tis a matter best known by few."

Mrs. Mather's eyes widened. "Do 'ee intend to break the law? To bring danger upon us all–upon our only child?"

"Hush, Lavinia," said Gran. Then she spoke to the man under the blanket. "We will keep 'ee safe." She stood up and said to the men, "Take him to the cabin."

"What if a Doane comes by?"

"Now, Vin," said Mr. Mather, "that's not likely in the middle of the night in this storm."

"What if a neighbor falls ill and sends for Gran?"

"Lavinia, heat up a bit of broth," said Gran. "He'll be fine in the cabin." She turned to Florence. "I'll need a basin of warm water. Fetch me the teakettle, will 'ee?"

As Mr. Mather and the teamster helped the ailing fugitive to his feet, the folds of the blanket fell back. Florence saw a dark, close-cropped head, and a glistening face the color of the coffee she served each morning. She saw a flash of white as the sick man's eyes caught hers, and felt a wave of fear as if his pain were her own.

Then Gran pulled the blanket back up over the man's head. She placed both her hands on his shoulders as if willing her own strength into him. "With the name Jonah," she said, "there's a remarkable journey behind and before 'ee."

"And the Maker's protection over 'ee," added Mr. Mather.

The men stepped out into the rain, with Gran close behind them.

In the kitchen, the silence deepened as Mrs. Mather stirred the broth, her head bent low over the pot. She did not look up as she said, "Take Gran that kettle and come back inside directly. Don't go near that man, Florence."

Through the steady rain, Florence carried the hot teakettle toward the narrow lighted windows of the cabin. On the porch, she reached for the latch and found to her dismay that the cabin door was locked. She rapped at the door. "Father?" she called. The door cracked open slightly, and Florence glimpsed two jars of preserves on the table, exactly as she had left them.

"Gran asked for hot water," she said.

"I'll take it to her," said Mr. Mather. After he disappeared inside, Florence listened to the murmur of voices from the other side of the door.

Then her father joined her on the porch, leaving the door ajar.

Florence ventured to ask, "What . . . what would happen if he were to be found?"

"If he's found out, he'll be taken back to the one who claims himself the poor fellow's master. I shouldn't like to think how an angry master might deal with a runaway."

At his answer Florence felt shame that her thoughts had dwelt so entirely on the danger to her own family that she had not been thinking about the fugitive's troubles at all. She remembered Katie playing at being Eliza, risking her life to cross the icy river to escape the dogs and men chasing her.

Mr. Mather looked at his daughter's troubled face. "But he'll not be found out. We Cornish have a long history of keeping secrets."

Banvard appeared at the door.

"How is he?" Mr. Mather asked.

"Your mother thinks he had too much sun and not enough to drink today. Only a chill, she says, from the sudden rain." Banvard ran a hand through his dark hair. "Unfortunately, the Chesapeake sails at dawn. I don't know when another of our own will arrive in harbor."

"Our own?" Florence asked.

"A ship whose captain assists in our cause," said Banvard. "A ship that will take Jonah to Canada and freedom." He turned to Mr. Mather. "Sir, I never intended to involve you or your family in this manner. When first we spoke, I thought only to make use of your inn as a staging-place. I hoped that on occasion I might leave a fresh team for the last leg of the journey to Racine."

"I am glad 'ee saw fit to trust us," said Mr. Mather.

He was about to say more when Mrs. Mather stepped onto the porch with a tray in her arms. "Here is the broth," she said. "Mister Banvard, I've brought 'ee some tea. And a plate of scones to go with the preserves my daughter made."

Mr. Mather moved forward to take the tray from her. "Bless 'ee, Vin."

Mrs. Mather sidestepped him and drew away from his outstretched arms. "I'll not have it said that travelers were ever made unwelcome at the Mather Inn."

Chapter 10

Independence Day

"Buggy's ready," called Thomas from the yard one fine July morning. "If we're to be in Rochester by noon, we'd best get moving!"

"Katie, take the quilt. Amos, you take the lunch basket," Ma ordered. "Now where's Matilda?"

Matilda entered the kitchen, carefully arranging a few curling tendrils around her face.

"Why've you done up your hair so fine?" Katie asked. "Having lemonade at the Union House isn't exactly another wedding dance."

"Oh, hush, Katie." Matilda swept ahead of the rest of them onto the porch.

"Who's going to mind the gate?" Katie asked as Pa handed her up into the buggy.

"It's Independence Day, Daughter. We'll leave the gate open for all who travel today."

The journey to Rochester took nearly two hours. Katie enjoyed the ride. The buggy wheels made a rhythmic hum as they rolled along the planks. Before the plank road was built a few years back, she had never even been to Rochester—the journey took much longer on a dirt road.

The sun was nearly overhead when the McEachrons pulled into the bustling village. Small houses lined each side of the main street. But on the east bank of the Fox River, Mr. Ela's huge white house with green shutters stood alone.

The buggy rolled over the bridge into the business side of town and drew up to the Union House, an enormous inn. Down the river, past the fanning mill and carriage factory, towered a large grist-mill.

Thomas pulled the horses up to a rail. "Don't go running off," Ma warned Amos and Katie. "Get the quilt and the basket, and we'll picnic first."

Along the river between the bridge and the factory, many families were spreading quilts on the grass. Katie and Amos spread theirs in the shade of a maple where they had a good view of the side door of Mr. Ela's factory. The speakers would stand on the stone steps of the factory. Nearby, the American flag flapped in the breeze. Ma and Matilda unpacked the fried chicken, black raspberry tarts, thick slices of bread and butter, and peas in the pod.

Thomas looked around. "Reckon I'll wander up Main Street."

"You'll sit and eat first," said Ma. "The horses will still be there to see in an hour."

Katie bit hungrily into a crispy drumstick. Her gaze scanned the gathering crowd. Pa and Ma nodded to familiar Yorkville faces and to others they recognized as regular travelers on the plank road.

Katie was eating her third tart when Amos called out, "There's Mister Banvard." Amos scrambled to his feet and ran over to the teamster. "Mister Banvard, would you show me the factory?"

The tall man smiled down at Amos and then peered over at the McEachron family. He nodded to Pa and Ma. Matilda barely looked up at him from beneath the brim of her hat.

"Mister Ela has allowed us to show the works today," said the teamster. "I'd be pleased to take Amos through."

"That's a kind offer," said Ma. "Perhaps after the speeches, Andrew and the boys will accompany you, while the girls and I go to the shops."

"I'll stop back then," said Mr. Banvard before strolling away.

A distinguished-looking man climbed the stone front steps of the factory. He held up a hand for silence, and the crowd quieted to listen. "On behalf of my townsmen," Richard Ela began, "I welcome all of you to Rochester on the anniversary of our Independence. This glorious day on which our freedom was declared is one we Americans must never forget. In honor of the occasion, Rochester's own schoolmaster will now recite the Declaration of Independence."

The schoolmaster was a pink-faced, balding man whose clothing seemed shabby next to Mr. Ela's fine attire. However, he possessed the same authority that Katie recognized in her own father and brother Will. When the fellow reverently took off his hat, hundreds of men in the park moved swiftly to do the same.

The schoolmaster's clear voice rang out over the crowd.

We hold these truths to be self-evident, that all men are created equal, that they are endowed by their Creator with certain unalienable rights . . .

The familiar words echoed across the hot July air. A shiver went down Katie's back as she realized that across this vast country, from New York all the way west to California, Americans would pause from their daily work to hear these words and mark this day.

After the recitation, Mr. Ela introduced the presidential speakers. Katie listened to speeches in support of Franklin Pierce, the Democratic nominee for president, and Winfield Scott, the Whig nominee. That was followed by a rousing campaign song to the tune of "Old Dan Tucker."

"Why isn't President Fillmore running, Pa?" Katie asked. "Isn't he a Whig?"

"He lost too many Northern votes when he passed the Fugitive Slave Law," said Pa. "The Whigs had to find a new candidate." He put a finger to his lips to shush her as Old Man Caswell climbed the steps to join Mr. Ela.

Old Man Caswell stood holding his hat in his hand. "Friends," he began, "I'm but a simple Cornishman. As my dear wife will tell 'ee, I'm more simple than most." The crowd chuckled in appreciation.

He continued, "I tell 'ee now, though, that this day of American independence belongs to me, too. The day belongs to all of us who crossed the sea to make a better life for ourselves and our children."

He lifted his square chin high. "And though I might not have been an American as long as some here, I've been a proud Wisconsinian longer than a few!"

The men and boys in the crowd roared their approval.

Old Man Caswell held his hat aloft. The crowd grew still. "As the good schoolmaster has reminded us, *all men are created equal*." His voice was deeper and grander now. "Brave men penned those words more than eighty years ago. Once a year we listen to those words and cheer, and our hearts are filled with satisfaction. With pride we walk among our fellow pioneers, confident that we will be accepted as their equals."

He paused and looked out over the river. "Here in Wisconsin we are secure in those *unalienable rights*. But elsewhere in this country, men are bought and sold."

Old Man Caswell placed one hand over his heart and looked searchingly at the crowd. "How can I enjoy my own liberty when other men are bound in chains? How can I be content to pursue my own happiness when other men are traded like cattle or potatoes? Slavery is an abomination to the very soul of our country!" His voice thundered across the river.

The statement was followed by scattered whistles and applause from the crowd. Then, a voice drawled from the edge of the gathering, "Do you claim that the Congress of the United States of America practices abomination? A fine citizen you are."

Another voice called, "There's slaves in the Holy Book itself! Do you call that an abomination?"

Katie rose from the ground to get a look at the men who had challenged Old Man Caswell. One was tall with a sunburnt face under dirty-blond hair and mustache. The other was stocky. Beside them stood Big Jim and Charlie Doane.

"How many of you folks are wearing cotton cloth today?" shouted the first man. "Without the work of the South, you'd have naught but wool to wear all summer."

"Can't raise cotton without slaves!" added Big Jim. "Ain't that right?" He turned to the men nearby, who nodded.

Suddenly the blacksmith Owen Caswell appeared next to the Doanes. "Let my grandfather speak," he said. His voice sounded very different from the cheerful man Katie knew.

"And why shouldn't I state my opinion, same as he does?" said Charlie Doane. He took a couple of wobbly steps toward Owen, fists clenched.

"They're going to fight!" said Amos.

Many in the crowd turned to watch the two men who stood with muscles flexed, staring at one another with angry eyes.

The blond stranger grinned. "Come on, Charlie. You can take him!" His words were slurred.

"Put him in his place!" cried the stocky man.

"I've no wish to fight with 'ee," said Owen. "I only ask that 'ee let my grandfather speak."

"He's scared!" said the stocky man.

"This has gone far enough," said Pa. "Thomas, come along."

Pa and Thomas quickly made their way toward the men. Ignoring her mother's voice, Katie hurried after them.

"Now, fellows," said Pa, taking Big Jim by the elbow, "let's talk about this."

Thomas said to Charlie Doane, "Where's Lightning? Are you ready to race? Isn't it time to get him out to the track?"

As the Doanes turned to answer the McEachrons, the two strangers disappeared into the crowd. Owen Caswell relaxed, and the other settlers turned back to the speaker.

Old Man Caswell quickly finished his speech and was met with a mixture of applause and catcalls. To Katie's delight, he passed his hat to take up a collection for the abolitionist society. She saw a number of settlers turn away from the hat, but many others dropped in coins.

None of the speeches that followed were as exciting as Old Man Caswell's. Katie grew drowsy from the heat as others praised Racine County's progress, and the success of the plank road that was helping to make Wisconsin a leading producer of the nation's wheat. Pa joined the Agricultural Society on the stage to speak of the county fair.

He and the society's president unrolled a broadside for the event. "Read about the prize listings at the Union House and Jackson's Mercantile," said the president, a signal that the speeches were over.

Quickly, the crowd began to disperse.

Mr. Banvard appeared as Katie helped Matilda fold the quilt. "Would you like to take a look at the factory now?" he asked Amos and Thomas.

"The girls and I will be going to Mister Jackson's store," Ma told Pa.

Matilda said suddenly, "I believe I'd like to see the factory."

Katie stared at her sister. "Whatever for? You've no interest in fanning mills."

"As an employee of the Plank Road Company, I ought to learn more about the most important products of Wisconsin."

Katie decided that Matilda had let the speeches go to her head. She opened her mouth to say so, but Ma took her by the hand. "Come along, Katie."

Katie and Ma made their way along the crowded street. Jackson's store was much bigger than Mr. Ives' place at the Grove. Straw hats, ribbons, stacks of yard goods, buttons and hairbrushes, butter churns, coffee, mixing bowls and tin pails were displayed on the shelves that lined the walls, floor to ceiling.

"We need cinnamon," Ma said. "And I ought to look at buttons. I do like to see a fine selection of goods." As they walked among the aisles, she added, "I was surprised you didn't invite Florence along for the day."

Katie did not care to talk about Florence. "'That's a fine bowl," she said. "Yours is so old and cracked."

Ma looked at the creamy yellow bowl with the brown stripes. "Have you quarreled with Florence?"

"Perhaps you should get a new bowl."

"You've not been over to the inn since you went strawberry picking," Ma said. "Nor has Florence come to call."

Katie studied the pottery display.

"A quarrel will not end a friendship," Ma said, "unless you let it."

"What if . . . what if I try to make things right, but she's not willing?" Katie ran her fingers around the smooth rim of the bowl.

Ma reached for the bowl. "I could buy a new one," she said. "Throw out the one with the chipped edge. But that bowl was chipped in the wagon coming west. Every time I use it, it brings back such memories. My mother gave that bowl to me when I married. I've kneaded bread and bathed babies in it. I've filled it with the harvest of our first garden in Wisconsin. I've watched my daughters learn to make spice cake the way my mother and her mother did. Even chipped as it is, that bowl brings memories worth more than any new one."

"So Florence is a chipped bowl?"

"So a friendship can endure hard use and become all the more precious."

Chapter 11

Fast Horses

Katie and Ma returned to the riverside just as the other McEachrons came back from their tour of the factory. Amos was still pestering Mr. Banvard with questions about the machinery, while Pa and Matilda followed along behind them. Meanwhile Thomas headed up toward the bridge.

"How was the factory?" Ma asked Amos as he flung himself onto the ground.

"You should have seen it! The very latest fanning mills separate the wheat kernels from the chaff by–"

"Where's Thomas going?" said Katie.

"The horse races," said Mr. Banvard. "That's where I'm headed."

Katie looked at Ma. "We're going over, too, aren't we?"

"It's dreadfully hot," Ma said. "Wouldn't you rather stay here by the river?"

"Big Jim Doane's Lightning will be a sight to see," said Amos.

Matilda said suddenly, "I'll take the children to the races."

Katie frowned. "We're not babies, Matilda. You needn't take us–"

"Go on, all of you!" interrupted Ma. "Just mind you're back in time for a lemonade at the Union House before the journey home."

"Where's your sorrel, Mister Banvard?" asked Amos. "Aren't you going to race?"

"I'm not much for a contest," said the teamster, "though I do appreciate fast horses and a bit of excitement now and then."

On the east end of Rochester, an open field on Mr. Ela's land was known as "the track." Whenever people gathered in town for an occasion, the men would eventually make their way to the track. To many of them, a man was judged as much by his horses as by his brains or his brawn or his land.

In the stifling heat, the crowd had ambled from the shady riverside to the field where only a few trees stood. When Amos saw Thomas standing in the field with Lightning and the Doanes, he ran on ahead. Mr. Banvard, Matilda, and Katie stopped under the nearest oak, where the Caswells and other Yorkville settlers were waiting.

Even at this distance Katie could hear Big Jim Doane's familiar boast, "Is there any question? Mine's the fastest horse here!" Then Big Jim saw the teamster. "Banvard! Where's that sorrel?"

"Weather's not fit for man or beast to run," Mr. Banvard called back with a smile. "I'll not be racing today."

"Takes more than hot air to keep a Doane from racing," said Big Jim.

"And little more than that to get one started, eh?" said Old Man Caswell to those nearby. The other settlers chuckled.

Big Jim said, "Come back on a cooler day, Banvard, I'll see you on a track."

Banvard shrugged his shoulders. "You might indeed. Good luck to you, sir."

Other riders took up Big Jim's challenge.

Owen Caswell stepped toward Katie and her sister, who was fanning herself with her hat. "Good day, Matilda," he said. "'Tis a hot one indeed." He looked at Mr. Banvard.

"Good afternoon, Owen." Matilda stopped fanning herself, but her face was still red.

"Are you acquainted with David Banvard?" she said. "He drives a wagon for Mister Ela. Mister Banvard, this is Owen Caswell, blacksmith in Yorkville."

Mr. Banvard extended his hand. "A pleasure to meet you," he said. "I know your grandfather. He comes to see Mister Ela on occasion."

"Aye, they're friends of old," said Owen.

Each of the two men sized up the other, just as Big Jim Doane or Thomas might size up a horse. Matilda was fanning herself again, her gaze fixed on the horses lining up along the track.

"Horses at the ready, men?" came the voice of Mr. Ela. "Hold the line now."

Katie studied the row of riders reining in their eager mounts. Charlie Doane, who was much lighter in weight than his father, was perched on Lightning.

Mr. Ela held his right hand high.

"Let's race!" he cried, dropping his arm.

Half a dozen horses shot out across the field. Twenty-four hooves pounded the turf as blacks and bays and chestnuts thundered along, necks outstretched and tails streaming behind. The riders flogged the horses with their hats as the crowd cheered them on.

"Go to it, Lightning!" shouted Big Jim Doane.

Without Ma there to stop her, Katie put two fingers in her mouth and whistled as loudly as any of the boys.

Even Matilda waved her hat as Doane's chestnut pounded down the stretch well ahead of the others.

"Fastest horse in the county!" Big Jim shouted, slapping the backs of Thomas and Amos and anybody else within reach. "Let's get him cooled down."

Owen glanced at Matilda. "I hadn't known 'ee were so fond of racing," he said with a smile. Mr. Banvard was watching Matilda, too.

Deftly Matilda positioned her hat over her tousled hair. "I do appreciate fast horses," she said, "and a bit of excitement now and then." She turned to Katie. "We ought to be meeting Ma and Pa at the Union House."

"Will 'ee be staying for the dance tonight?" Owen asked. "I could bring 'ee home afterward."

Matilda's eyes were hidden once more under the brim of her hat. "No, I thank you. I won't be able to stay," she said. She nodded to the blacksmith and the teamster. "Good day to you, Owen. And to you, Mister Banvard."

A few minutes later when Katie stepped inside the Union House, she felt immediately the drop in temperature within the thick stone walls. The lemonade that Pa ordered for them was deliciously refreshing, tart and sweet all at once.

"To think of having real lemonade twice in one summer," said Katie. "Wouldn't it be wonderful to drink lemonade every day?"

Matilda lifted her chin. "I shouldn't like to turn something special into something ordinary," she said.

July 5, 1852

Today we went to Rochester to enjoy the Independence Day festivities. Independence Day was actually yesterday, a Sunday, so the gathering was today.

Ma thought I might have invited Florence to come along. We have not spoken since our strawberry fight. Perhaps I will invite her along the next time I go on an excursion. She would prove better company than Thomas and Amos!

Chapter 12

Friends of Emerson

I n the hot and crowded schoolroom, Florence stood on the platform beside the teacher's desk. "The piece that I have chosen to recite is 'The Apology' by Ralph Waldo Emerson," she said. "In this poem, Mister Emerson shows us that an artist draws from the land just as a farmer does. I think he wants us to see that a poet does important work, just as an innkeeper . . . or a blacksmith does."

Florence took a deep breath and began, keeping her eyes fixed on a point somewhere just above the heads of the men standing at the back of the schoolroom.

When she finished the last stanza:

> One harvest from thy field
> Homeward brought the oxen strong;
> A second crop thine acres yield
> Which I gather in a song.

and bowed her head, she was startled at the rousing burst of applause. Among the blur of faces she saw Gran's shining eyes and her father's smile. She did not see her mother, though.

"Thank you, Florence," said Miss Waite. "Our final speaker today will be Katherine McEachron. Katie has prepared an original oration."

Katie stood up as Florence returned to her seat. They both

averted their eyes. As Florence folded her hands in her lap to listen to Katie, she wondered why her mother had not come to what might be her last summer Recitation Day.

"When our forefathers declared their independence," Katie began, "they said that *all men are created equal.* People have come to the United States of America from many countries precisely because of these proclaimed freedoms. It is time for us, as Americans, to embrace that freedom. If we all are truly created equal, are not black men as worthy as white? How then do we allow slavery in the United States of America, where people have fought and died for the cause of freedom?

"We may buy and sell horses or sheep or cattle–but why do we put black men and women and children on such a level?"

While the Caswells nodded, the Doanes and a few others in the schoolhouse fidgeted and looked uncomfortable. From her seat, Florence could not see how the McEachrons reacted to their daughter's words, but she suspected from the teacher's surprised look that Katie had diverged from the script approved by Miss Waite.

"How can we support slavery," Katie continued boldly, "when we declare that all men are created equal? If we are truly Americans, we would do everything in our power to free those who are treated as animals, not as humans, under the law. Let us be ever vigilant to erase the blot that slavery has brought upon our nation–"

"Thank you, Katie," Miss Waite cut in. "You have stated your position quite clearly. You may be seated."

Katie marched back to her desk, then slumped in her seat. Florence felt another flash of anger at her old friend. As always, Katie McEachron thought she knew everything. But did she know what it was like to sit behind closed curtains in a small cabin, listening to the weary voice of a fugitive telling his tale?

Florence remembered the early morning after David Banvard had brought the escaped slave Jonah to the Mathers the night of the rainstorm. Hunched at the hearth in the cabin, Jonah had kept his eyes intent upon his whittling, dropping bits of wood shavings into the ashes. Following Gran's instructions, Florence had stitched a row of coins into the hem of one of Granfer's old shirts. A long scrap of cloth tucked alongside separated the coins and kept them from clinking.

"My girl Hattie could sew a fine seam," Jonah said. "She 'bout the size of young miss here when she been sold away. Her mama and me never see her no mo'."

Florence looked up in horror. "Never?"

"No, miss. Master, he say a young lady buy her. He say my girl won' do no field work, no suh. He say my girl gonna be a fine lady's maid. I hope dat so."

Jonah was gone by sun-up, but his words remained with Florence.

Miss Waite stepped onto the platform. She thanked the neighbors for coming to Recitation Day. Little Daniel Doane handed Miss Waite a bedraggled bouquet, and the settlers applauded the teacher and pupils again. Summer term was over.

Outside the schoolhouse, the women clustered to praise their neighbors' children. Most of the men started for the waiting wagons and buggies, eager to return to the hayfields during the stretch of dry weather. Mr. McEachron took time to say, "Florence, I am glad indeed that you introduced Emerson's ideas to Yorkville."

Gran kissed Florence's cheek. "Granfer would have been so proud."

Mr. Mather wrapped his arms around the two of them. "Nary a Mather in all of Cornwall ever spoke so fine."

"Where's Mother?" asked Florence.

Mr. Mather whistled through his teeth. "She took a spill on the back stairs. Twisted her ankle. I promised her a private recitation upon our return."

Back at the inn, Florence hung her bonnet beside the kitchen door and hurried to the little room where her mother sat in the bed, her bound foot propped on a pillow.

Gran brought in a tray and set it next to the bed. "I talked to the McEachrons after the recitations," she said, "and engaged Matilda to help out while 'ee mend."

"Oh! We can't have a McEachron here," said Mrs. Mather. "With her father a justice of the peace? What if she caught wind of . . . the midnight packages?"

Gran smiled as she poured out the tea. "Matilda is hardly one to meddle where she doesn't belong."

Mrs. Mather shook her head. "I have no complaint against our neighbors. My only complaint is that I must lie helpless while others do my work. I warn 'ee, I cannot bear this long."

Gran clucked her tongue. "Sit 'ee back now, and listen to Florence."

Florence stood in the middle of the room and began to recite. When she got to the lines:

> Chide me not, laborious band,
> For the idle flowers I brought;
> Every aster in my hand
> Goes home loaded with a thought.

she glimpsed a hint of a smile on her mother's face.

Matilda was quick to fit into the rhythm of life at the Mather Inn, starting with the early breakfasts for departing teamsters eager to be on the road before the heat of the day. When the sun was high overhead and new wagons began to pull into the yard, Matilda worked willingly at the wood stove in the sweltering kitchen. Her face glowing with exertion, she carried steaming platters out to the farmers and their sons taking surplus hay to sell in Racine.

Even Mrs. Mather said grudgingly that Mrs. McEachron had trained her daughter well.

Florence enjoyed the conversations in the kitchen. For the first time in her life, she had a friend who enjoyed reading as much as she did, and Matilda was generous in loaning volumes from the McEachron collection.

One day over the dishes, Matilda said, "I've had a special fondness for Emerson since the day I was reading outside the tollhouse, and a teamster said to me:

> *Books are among the best of things, well used—*
> *Abused, among the worst.*

Matilda laughed. "A teamster quoting Emerson! I asked where on earth he came from, and do you know what he told me?"

Florence shook her head.

Matilda's eyes shone with merriment. "Again, more Emerson!

> *Go where he will, the wise man is at home,*
> *His hearth the earth; his hall the azure dome.*

"And I said, 'The *wise* man, yes . . . but where is a man like *you* at home?'" She pushed back a loose strand of hair. "He laughed, bowed, and gave me a harness bell as a token of victory."

One evening, when Florence was on the porch shaking out the broom, she heard a clatter of hooves on the plank road. A wagon approached the inn at a quicker pace than usual for weary horses at end of day. David Banvard pulled into the yard, reined in at the watering trough, and began to unharness the lathered horses from a wagon piled high with bundles.

"Good evening, Mister Banvard," Florence said. "Will 'ee take supper with us?"

"No, I thank you, Florence. I left a fresh team here so I might deliver these goods to the harbor without delay." His words were lightly spoken, but he gazed intently at her. "I'll take along a pasty, if I might. And perhaps you'd be so kind as to wrap a few more for any who might be in need." He nodded toward the wagon bed.

"And who might that be?"

Florence turned to see Matilda standing at the corner of the inn, a basket of greens in her hand.

"Miss McEachron!" said the teamster.

"Good evening, Mister Banvard."

After a long pause the teamster said, "I did not look to find you here."

Matilda smiled. "Then where *did* you look to find me?"

"I mean . . . I expected to see you at the tollgate."

"Are you so disappointed to see me here instead?" Matilda began to walk toward the wagon.

"Indeed not, Miss McEachron." The teamster took a few steps forward, to stand between Matilda and the wagon.

"Then what's in that wagon that won't keep till you've had an evening meal?"

"Nothing, Miss McEachron. That is, I mean, nothing that won't keep." David Banvard looked helplessly at Florence.

Florence was gripping her broom so tightly that her hands ached. "Matilda McEachron!" she burst out. "We didn't take on a hired girl to dally with teamsters! What would Owen Caswell think? Have 'ee no shame?"

Matilda's face flushed scarlet. She dropped the basket of greens and fled from the yard.

Chapter 13

Patches

Katie had come downstairs that same morning to find her brother Will sipping tea in the kitchen with Ma. "I've been waiting for you," he said.

"Whatever for?" Katie asked, wondering what she might have done wrong or forgotten to do.

Will grinned. "Don't look so fretful," he said. "I want only to borrow you for the day. Grace could use your help with a sewing project."

Ma glanced at Katie. "Perhaps Matilda or I ought to help out."

Will kept his eyes on his teacup. "Ma, she asked for Katie's company."

"May I go, Ma?"

After another anxious glance at Will, Ma nodded.

"She'd like you to bring the scraps from your red dress," said Will.

Eagerly Katie began spooning up her oatmeal. "Once I've collected eggs I'll get the scraps and be over directly."

"I'll gather those eggs," said Will. His chair scraped the plank floor as he pushed himself away from the table.

"Oh, dear," said Ma after the door slammed shut. "I didn't mean . . . I only thought that . . . you struggle so with your sewing. . . ."

Katie looked at her mother with indignation. "I learned from you. You might have taught me better!" Setting her bowl and spoon in the dry-sink with a clatter, she stomped out the door, almost knocking over Amos, who was bringing in the milk.

"Will and Katie are both looking a mite ornery today," Amos said cheerfully as he sat down to his breakfast.

Katie skipped through the orchard toward Will and Grace's house. Chickens and ducks pecked in the barnyard. Herbs and flowers in tidy beds adorned the kitchen garden alongside the porch, where Grace sat waiting.

"Sit 'ee down," said Grace. "I'm so anxious to show 'ee what I've done." She reached into her sewing basket and pulled out a piece of green calico. "Remember when 'ee told me about your idea for a Strawberry Patch quilt? I've made a pattern."

Grace pulled her chair closer. "I folded the fabric into quarters, cut out the shape, and opened it. Do 'ee see? Strawberry leaves!"

Katie gasped. "They're so beautiful!"

"And here are the strawberries." Grace unfolded a piece of brown fabric that formed four strawberry shapes. "Only I hadn't any red."

"I brought my scraps," said Katie, pulling the crimson calico from her basket. "May I cut out the strawberries?"

"We must cut ever so carefully," said Grace. "I've a mind to exhibit this quilt at the fair."

In Grace's kitchen, Katie folded a crimson fabric square into quarters before cutting out the strawberry shape. When she unfolded it, four berries were connected to one another. After she and Grace finished cutting the pieces, they returned to the porch to begin stitching the designs onto muslin squares.

"I'm glad to be doing the simple design of the fruit," Katie said as she watched Grace turning under all the jagged edges of the leaves.

Grace laughed. "I'm glad there's more red than green. 'Ee must show Florence your strawberry square."

Katie blushed. "I don't believe she'd care to see any more strawberries."

"Why not?" Grace asked. "Have 'ee quarreled?"

Katie nodded. "The day we made jam."

"But that was near a month ago! Surely an apology could put an end to it."

Katie kept her eyes on her sewing. "I've hardly seen her since Recitation Day. With her ma's ankle gone bad, I reckon she's quite busy at the inn."

"Recitation Day. That was quite a day for 'ee," Grace said with a smile.

Katie sighed. "I got extra chores on the last day of summer term as well as the first. Why should Pa have punished me for speaking my mind? Your grandfather says whatever he pleases."

"In his homeland, he dared not speak out against those in authority. He cherishes that right in this country."

"Then why can't I do the same?"

"Pa McEachron is the justice of the peace. He has sworn to follow the laws of the country. How does it look for his daughter to speak out against those laws?"

Katie had not thought of that. "Do you suppose Pa thinks slavery is just?"

"In all the years 'ee have lived under his roof," said Grace, "what has he taught 'ee?"

Katie continued to stitch, thinking the answer was not so

clear cut as the strawberry she was sewing.

Later that afternoon, when Katie returned to the farmhouse, Ma said, "Katie, run up and ask Missus Mather if Matilda might come home early. We've not had her with us at table for so long."

"The pasture will be full of mosquitoes," said Katie, looking for a reason not to go.

"Then walk along the road," said Ma, nudging her out the door.

Katie walked out to the road and up the embankment. She dawdled along the center of the road, her left foot up on the planks and her right foot down on the dirt lane—*clop thwump, clop thwump*—as she and Florence used to walk when they were young. Maybe she would apologize to Florence this very day. She hastened up to the inn yard to see Florence standing on the porch, broom in hand. Mr. Banvard stood in front of his wagon near the watering trough, with Matilda just a few steps away.

Katie was about to call out when she heard Florence declare, in a shrill and unnatural voice: ". . . to dally with teamsters! What would Owen Caswell think? Have 'ee no shame?"

Matilda dashed past Katie, her face as red as a strawberry.

July 31, 1852

To think that I was about to apologize to Florence for my poor behavior when I heard her scold Matilda so rudely! I didn't say a word to her or Mr. Banvard, but turned and followed Matilda home for supper.

I've never heard Florence speak in such a way. What is happening at the Inn?

Chapter 14

A Knock at the Door

Florence tossed in her bed. Was she awake or dreaming? A midnight parcel. The dark face of a fugitive in the kitchen. A knock at the door, and frantic voices.

With a start Florence sat up. The voices continued.

Through the window open to the late August night, she heard her mother. "How could 'ee be such a fool as to bring this trouble upon us?" and a responding murmur from her father.

Then a third voice. David Banvard.

Florence slipped out of bed and knelt at the window. Three figures stood in the darkness outside the kitchen door.

". . . how long they've been about," Banvard was saying, "but it's certain they've had their eyes on me. I dare not try to outrun men on horseback."

"So we're to have slave catchers and a federal marshal as our guests." Mrs. Mather's voice was angry. "Have 'ee any other such welcome company to announce?"

"No, ma'am," came the weary reply, "none but Hannah and little Johnny."

"Johnny?" said Mrs. Mather. The tone of her voice changed. "The child's name is Johnny?"

Mr. Mather's voice cut in. "Take them to the cabin. I'll see to the horses."

Florence hurried down the back stairs to the kitchen. Mrs. Mather was arranging a platter of cinnamon twists on a tray with two tin mugs. When Florence pattered into the room, shivering in her thin nightgown, her mother did not look up. "What brings 'ee downstairs?" she said.

"I heard Mister Banvard. Are slave catchers truly on his trail?" Florence felt a tightening deep inside as she waited for the answer.

"Such may be the last guests of the Mather Inn." Florence watched her mother slice a hunk of cheese and place two rolled napkins on the tray. Then Mrs. Mather looked up to gaze somewhere beyond her daughter.

"Wrap a cloak about 'ee," she said, "there's a chill in the air tonight. Take the tray to the cabin. I've something to fetch."

Florence carried the tray across the dark yard and climbed the low step to the cabin door. Only the narrowest thread of light escaped the shuttered windows.

"Gran?" she called. She heard the rattle of the latch, and then the door swung open to let her inside.

In the lamplight she saw the fugitives standing at the hearth. A tall woman with a faded green kerchief tightly bound around her head had her hands on the shoulders of a slender child. Gran beckoned the travelers to the table as if inviting them to tea.

"Hannah," Gran spoke to the woman, "this is my grand-daughter Florence. Florence, our guests are Miz Hannah and her son John. Here, child, have a cinnamon twist."

The boy ate the doughnut eagerly and gulped the milk.

"Johnny!" said the woman. "Mind yo' manners!" She smiled apologetically at Gran. "He's powerful hungry."

When she heard her father's whistle, Florence stepped to the door. He and David Banvard were standing outside. Gran joined them on the porch.

"Were the worst to happen," murmured Mr. Mather, "where

ought they to go?"

"Alton would help us," Gran said.

"Caswell's views are too widely known," said Banvard, his face strained and tight. "I'll not have him—or his family—endangered on my account."

"When the marshal comes riding," said Mr. Mather, "I'd like that pair well away from my property."

"Strawberry Glen!" said Florence suddenly. The others turned to look at her. "I . . . I know a shelter near the creek. On the McEachron land."

Mr. Mather looked at Gran and said slowly, "Neither a slaver nor a marshal's posse would suspect a justice of the peace."

"To the inn with 'ee both," Gran said to the two men. "Sit at table and tell Lavinia to serve 'ee long and leisurely."

Before the men strode off the porch, Florence saw her father reach for something leaning against the cabin wall. The gleaming barrel of the rifle startled her.

"Ah, there's nary a thing to worry about. Just get them safe to the glen," said Mr. Mather in a steady voice.

Gran and Florence stepped back inside the cabin, where the woman had already picked up her bundle. She stood alert and ready, looking to Gran for instructions. The boy's solemn face wore a faint milky moustache. With one hand he clutched at his mother's worn coat.

There came swift footsteps on the porch. In a flash, Mrs. Mather was inside the door. She stood before the woman and child, clutching a small bundle, gasping a bit to catch her breath. Then she leaned to look into the boy's face. "Are 'ee named Johnny?" she asked.

The boy stared at her wide-eyed, nodded, and took a step closer to his mother.

"Here's something to keep 'ee warm." Mrs. Mather held out the bundle, a small quilt with squares of soft greens and gray-blue. "I made this when Florence was a baby." She looked at the boy's mother. "I kept saving it for the next one. Three times I folded it away."

"Bless you, ma'am." The woman nudged her son forward, and he reached to take the bundle.

"For me?" he asked in a soft voice. The quilt fell open and he ran his hand across the colorful squares. "Thank you, ma'am," he said with a smile so wide that Florence and Gran could not help but smile, too.

For a moment his small hands touched Mrs. Mather's across the folded quilt.

"Godspeed, young John," whispered Mrs. Mather. She turned and left the cabin as swiftly as she had come.

Gran said, "Florence will lead 'ee to a place of shelter for the night." She held up one of the cinnamon twists. "'Tis the sign. Trust the one who comes to 'ee with this. " She thrust the other doughnuts and the last of the cheese into a napkin, tied off the corners, and handed it to the woman. "The Maker keep 'ee."

Out on the porch the woman whispered, "Now, Johnny, we's going to follow young miss into the fields again. How must we be?"

"We must be quiet as mice," the boy whispered back.

Florence pulled up the hood of her cloak and led the fugitives around back of the cabin under the oaks. In a moment the slope of the garden path hid them from sight of the inn. When she glanced behind, she could see David Banvard leading his horse Fancy toward the cabin. Florence picked her way along the hayfield, where the stubble scratched her bare ankles.

At the section-line road she looked left and right, though

she knew how unlikely were the chances of a late-night traveler. "Quick now!" she whispered. The three darted across the twin wheel ruts to the McEachron land on the other side.

The wheat shone deep and golden in the moonlight. Florence dared not lead them through the field, for the bent stalks would show their passage. Instead she continued north in the long prairie grass. How many mornings and afternoons had she walked this route with Katie and Amos, carefree and unthinking, in sunshine or snow?

Again Florence glanced back toward the inn. She could dimly see the tops of the oaks dark against the starry sky. At any moment the sounds of men on horseback might rise out of that grove. Florence quickened her pace.

Ahead loomed the tree line that marked the creek. Behind her she could hear the woman's breathing, and once the boy yipped softly as he stumbled in the dark. Florence wondered whether they felt the same fear that she did, and how many nights they had stayed just a few steps ahead of being captured. The woman's calm face at the cabin had reflected none of the fear Florence now felt. But surely they knew how much danger they faced.

Now the three of them disappeared into the shadows of the trees along the creek. At first Florence could not find the path through the brambles. Finally she pushed under an overhanging branch, and the track became familiar again. How often had she and Katie crept noiselessly along this trail, pretending that they were explorers or Indians or fugitives themselves?

The memory of those playful times steadied Florence's nerves.

"Here we must cross the creek," she said. She lifted the hem of her nightgown and made her way onto the stepping stones. "It isn't deep," she called softly, turning to look behind her.

"Follow my steps, Johnny."

Holding his mother's hand, the child stepped from one stone to the next. Florence had never felt more sure of her footing, as if her own steps were being guided. On the far bank Florence saw the vine-covered bower under which she and Katie had played for so many summers. She pushed aside the trailing vines and ducked to enter the shelter. "It's almost always dry inside," she said, "and well hidden from the world."

Under the canopy of branches, Florence and the woman had to stoop, but the boy could stand upright. "Please sit down," said Florence, hearing the echo of her mother's voice in her own. In the darkness she heard the woman and child sink down onto the carpet of leaves.

"Rest easy," Florence said. "Only Katie and I know of this place. When I was a child, my friend and I often came here to play."

"Young miss, I hope you still finds time to play. My Johnny need a chance to be a chile. Don't want him old and wore out before his time."

Dimly Florence saw the woman wrap the quilt around her son and hug him close. "Young miss, this crick run to a big river?"

"Granfer once told me it flows into the Root River. And then into Lake Michigan."

"Lake Michigan. That's where we headed, ain't it? Freedom on the other side."

"Yes, but it's a long way to the harbor," said Florence. "You must wait here. We'll send help for 'ee."

"Gonna wait one day for somebody come with the sign," the woman said. "Ain't nobody come by next nightfall . . . me and Johnny'll follow this crick on our own. Bless you, young miss!"

The journey back to the inn seemed longer than the flight to Strawberry Glen. Now that Florence was alone in the night, she began to tremble at the thoughts that assailed her. What if even now the marshal and the slave catchers were searching the inn? She tried to assure herself that a federal marshal, like a justice of the peace, was sworn to uphold the law. Yet slave catchers were bounty hunters, brutal men who made a living from the misfortunes of others. What if her father tried to resist them?

Florence told herself that had there been any gunfire, she would have heard it. The night was blessedly quiet as she crossed the road and walked swiftly across the hay stubble. The garden path took her up the slope to the cabin. Florence was startled by large eyes looking at her in the moonlight behind the cabin.

When she saw that it was Fancy, tied to a young oak behind the cabin, Florence stood still, to let her heart slow its frantic pounding and her breath come more steadily.

Pushing back her hood, she listened as hard as she could. Beyond the frogs and crickets came the whicker and stomp of horses—too close to be stabled in the log barn across the inn yard.

Cautiously Florence pulled up her hood again and stepped out from behind the cabin to glimpse the yard.

Lamplight from the windows of the inn's dining room spilled out in long pale rectangles into the yard where three saddled horses stood at the hitching rail.

She drew back close to the cabin wall, then tapped softly at the window. In a moment Gran's face appeared. "Slip round and come inside," Gran said. "We will let them think us long abed."

Quickly Florence stole around to the cabin porch, where Gran opened the door just wide enough to let her in.

"Is it the marshal?" whispered Florence. "Are they slavers? What's become of them inside?"

"Into bed with 'ee, and I'll tell all."

Obediently Florence climbed into bed, and Gran got in beside her. Again Florence thought of the early days and nights in the cabin. After Granfer died, she and Gran became bed-fellows. Many a night Gran had lain beside her, telling stories of the old country till Florence dropped off to sleep.

Now Gran had a new tale to tell. "They rode up not a quarter-hour after 'ee'd gone. Two of the men began poking about the log barn. The third went directly to the porch door and announced himself as Marshal Carter. Then one of the others comes quick from the barn. 'He's here,' says he to the marshal. 'I know his team. Banvard is here!'"

Gran chuckled. "And your father John says all cheery like, 'Is it David Banvard 'ee mean? What rare luck to have his friends stopping, too! Come in and share a late supper.' The marshal called the other men to the porch and they started inside. But your mother says, 'Marshal or no, I'll thank 'ee to wipe those boots before setting foot in my dining room.'"

Florence smiled, but her anxiety returned. "Miz Hannah said she'd wait only one day before moving on. How will Mister Banvard ever be able to get them to Racine?"

Gran shook her head. "I don't see that he will."

Chapter 15

Reluctant Hosts

The next morning, after a troubled sleep, when Florence brought the coffeepot to the dining room, three men were at breakfast. David Banvard sat with the two slave catchers who had followed him to the inn the night before. At the sound of fresh hoofbeats in the yard, they all looked up. Marshal Carter entered the dining room with Charlie Doane and Jasper Everett behind him.

"'Morning, Miss Mather," said the marshal to Florence. "My deputies and I will take some breakfast, if you please."

Florence stepped into the kitchen, where her mother was already filling the plates with sausage, fried potatoes, and gravy. As she set the plates in front of the newcomers, the nearest slave catcher fixed her with sharp eyes.

"Now, missy, do you know what sin is?" he asked.

"Yes, sir," said Florence. She kept her eyes on the steaming coffee she was pouring for Charlie.

"Then your ma and pa must have taught you to tell the truth. Ain't that so, missy?"

"Yes, sir." Florence felt her cheeks growing warm.

"Now you know what happens to folks who don't tell the truth, don't you?"

Florence did not respond. The man leaned closer, and she could smell his sour breath. "They burn in Hell, missy," he said. "They burn in Hell."

The marshal cleared his throat. "Let the child alone, Danford."

The other man spoke. "Aye, Danford, anybody but a fool could tell she ain't no lawbreaker." He smiled at Florence. "Your folks are good people, ain't they?"

"Yes, sir."

"You all just want to help other folks, ain't that right?"

Florence hesitated. "Yes, sir."

"And that Mister Banvard, he just wants to help other folks, too." The man's eyes held hers as he nodded and smiled again. Florence found herself nodding with him.

From the corner of her eye she could see David Banvard steadily spooning up his gravy, though she was sure he could not be tasting a single mouthful.

The stranger continued with a casual drawl, "Now, ain't that why he brings black folks on through heah?"

The teamster set down his spoon. All six men looked at Florence and waited for a reply.

Florence remembered Gran's wide eyes and timid voice outside the Ives Grove store, on a day that seemed so long ago.

"Black folks?" she whispered. "Faith 'n' truth, sirs, I'd be much afraid of black folks."

David Banvard stood up. "Accusations scarcely aid the appetite," he said. "Good day to you, Florence."

"Going to hitch your wagon, Banvard?" said Danford. "Where are you bound? Care for some company along the way?"

The marshal spoke firmly. "It's not any business of yours where he's bound. I've got a posse gathering to find the missing fugitives."

"Still," said the other man, "no law says we can't take the

116

same road. Ain't that right, Marshal?"

Danford and the other man were rising from their seats when Gran appeared in the doorway. "David," she called, "Will 'ee have savory or sweet? Come and choose a pasty."

"Yes, ma'am." The teamster followed her into the kitchen.

Behind him Danford peered through the doorway. When he saw Banvard follow Gran out the back door, he stepped into the kitchen.

Mrs. Mather stepped back from the stove, a steaming skillet in one hand, a wooden spoon in the other. "Have 'ee had sufficient, Mister Danford? I've another batch of fried potatoes."

"No, thank you, ma'am," said the man. He attempted to move past her to the back door, but the hot skillet blocked his path.

"Have 'ee tried a cinnamon twist? Florence, fetch the crock, will 'ee?"

Immediately Florence picked up the crock from the shelf and stood beside her mother. She smiled at the slave catcher. "Cinnamon twists are Mother's specialty," she said. "Mind 'ee, they're not proper Cornish."

"Missy, I ain't got time for doughnuts. Pardon me, ma'am." Abruptly he turned and strode through the dining room and out the door.

Florence looked at her mother, who was looking back at her, a rare glint of humor in her eyes. "'Mind 'ee,'" Mrs. Mather said in a mincing voice, "'they're not proper Cornish.'" She chuckled as she returned the skillet to the stove.

A few minutes later the entire Mather family stood at the teamster's wagon. David Banvard had led his team up to the watering trough. A morning fog lay over the yard, shrouding Marshal Carter, his posse, and the slave catchers standing on the porch. Florence wondered what Gran and the teamster had said to one another during the brief moment they had snatched together.

"Florence! Florence Mather!" a voice called from through the fog. Katie McEachron came around the corner of the inn. Oblivious to the strangers on the porch, she went straight to Florence and clasped both her hands. "Florence, I am so sorry we quarreled. It was all my fault. I was stupid and childish, and I do hope you'll forgive me."

She turned to Mrs. Mather. "Please, won't you let Florence ride to Racine with us? We're taking our wool to market today. Pa said I could ask whether Florence might come along!"

Danford and his partner stepped off the porch. Together, the two slave catchers approached the wagon.

"Young lady," Danford said, "do you know this man?" He pointed to Banvard.

Katie stared at the men. "Why, certainly I know Mister Banvard," she said. "Why shouldn't I?" She looked from one to the other.

Danford stooped to look into Katie's face intently. "And do you know why this man comes 'round heah so often?"

"Indeed I do," said Katie. She seemed to enjoy the attention of her audience. "Mister Banvard is conducting business that he oughtn't."

The marshal, Charlie Doane, and Jasper Everett moved closer to listen. "And what business would that be?"

The teamster's face went absolutely still.

Katie tossed her head and looked triumphantly at the tall man. "Mister Banvard thinks it's his business to court my sister!"

Chapter 16

A Dangerous Journey

Katie was pleased to see that Mr. Banvard looked rightfully embarrassed. Charlie Doane and Jasper Everett broke out laughing.

"So, Danford," said the marshal. "Perhaps you're chasing someone for the wrong reason!"

Danford and his stocky partner, who both looked vaguely familiar to Katie, shook their heads and scowled at the marshal. "He's up to no good," said Danford to the marshal. "And we'll find them folks that he hid."

"We've followed him all the way from Janesville," said the stocky man. "We're not going to lose him now."

"This is *my* territory," said the marshal. "The boys and I can take it from here."

Katie looked around. Banvard had disappeared. A moment later, a sound of hoofbeats erupted from behind Gran's cabin. Banvard and his sorrel mare lit out from the mist under the oaks and headed toward the plank road.

"He'll get away!" shouted Danford.

"Not from me," said Charlie, swinging aboard his horse. He and Jasper galloped out of the yard while Danford and his partner ran toward the barn.

Katie gaped at the marshal, wondering what astonishing thing might happen next.

"Katie," said Gran abruptly, "Fortune has certainly brought 'ee here. We've a mind to go to Racine ourselves. We can easily take the McEachron wool. Florence and I will be over within the hour to fetch 'ee."

Gran turned to Florence. "I expect Katie needs a cinnamon twist. Take her to the kitchen, will 'ee?"

"But, Gran—" Katie's protest ended as Florence took her hand and pulled her up the porch steps and on through the dining room into the kitchen.

Katie said, "I do so regret not asking you to go to Rochester on Independence Day. I'm sorry I waited so long to—"

"Katie, please listen! We need help—we've lives to save."

"What . . . what do you mean?"

"We've hidden—" Florence looked around and lowered her voice, "We've hidden two fugitives and must take them to the harbor."

"Fugitives?" said Katie in bewilderment.

Two bright spots of color stood in Florence's cheeks. "Runaways, Katie. Slaves. A woman and child."

"Runaway slaves? Why, Florence Mather!" Sudden recognition dawned in Katie's mind. "That Danford man . . . I saw him on Independence Day," she whispered. "Is he a slaver? But how did runaways ever come here? You'll be in awful trouble if you're caught—"

"Katie, do keep still! I need 'ee to go to Hannah and Johnny. They're at Strawberry Glen." Florence held a cinnamon twist right up to Katie's nose. "'Tis the sign," she said. "Tell them to follow the creek east to the fork and take the south branch to the bridge at the plank road. They're to wait in the long grass till we come."

She pressed a napkin full of cinnamon twists into Katie's hand. "Hurry, Katie. Take the message and get home quick as 'ee can. Gran and I'll fetch 'ee there within the hour."

Katie opened her mouth to speak and found herself completely without words.

Florence pushed her toward the door. "On Recitation Day, someone said we ought to do everything in our power," she said. "Will 'ee please begin now?"

Katie took the cinnamon twists and stepped out the back door. With a sudden sense of urgency, she picked up her skirts and ran through the oaks.

Though the morning was foggy, Katie had no trouble making her way along the familiar path. Just outside Strawberry Glen, she paused and listened. Hearing nothing, she approached the fallen tree, pushed aside the grapevines, and peered into the shelter. A dark face stared back at her.

For a moment the woman eyed Katie in silence. Then she said, "Beggin' pardon, miss. I's just passing through. Took shelter for the night, but I be on my way soon."

Then Katie remembered the doughnuts wrapped in the napkin. Dropping to her knees, she said, "Oh, but aren't you Miz Hannah? Where's Johnny?" She tried to peer over the woman's shoulder. "I'm Katie. I'm here to help. I've brought cinnamon twists." She opened the napkin.

"Praise be," said the woman, a smile of relief breaking out on her face. "Come on out, Johnny."

A quick little hand darted out to snatch a doughnut, and then a child's face appeared, grinning around the cinnamon twist.

"Miz Hannah, we'll get you to the harbor this day," Katie said. She explained the Mathers' plan.

"Is the crick wooded? Be there houses 'long the way?"

"It's mostly wooded. Runs through the back forties. Just fields and pastures. Where there aren't any trees, the grass should be long enough to hide you."

"I's good at crawlin' through grass," said the boy.

"Are you, Johnny? What else are you good at?" asked Katie.

"Keepin' still so nobody find me. Mama tell me there be time to keep silence and time to speak."

Katie nodded. "That's just what my pa tells me."

She pulled the grapevines back while Hannah and Johnny stepped out from the bower. "My, but you're tall," Katie said, as Hannah stood up straight. "Near as tall as an oak sapling. And your skin is beautiful. It's the color of Ma's chestnut brocade. She wore it to Will's wedding back in June." Katie smiled down at Johnny. "I've never met real colored folks before."

Hannah chuckled. "We's real as they come, Miss Katie."

"Oh, nobody calls me that. Just Katie, that's all."

Katie saw the two safely on their way toward the bridge and then hurried home, avoiding the temptation of cutting across the wheat field. She would catch it from Pa if she damaged the crop so close to harvest.

She found her father out in the barn, where he was tying the mouth of a bulging wool sack. "Pa," she said, trying to keep her voice as matter-of-fact as possible, "Gran Mather said she'd take me and the wool to Racine today. Isn't that fine? You need not miss a day's work."

Pa straightened up from his task. "Daughter, the Mathers need not do the McEachrons' work."

"Oh no, Pa! I can do the McEachrons' work. I'm able, Pa. I know to barter for a good price at the market and record the weight and make sure we're paid proper."

"You and I will take the wool to market."

"But, Pa, Gran said she'd do it. She's to come within the hour."

Pa frowned. "No more of this. Go ready yourself for the journey." He turned back to his work.

Katie was on the porch, a covered basket in hand, her face scrubbed clean and hair freshly plaited, when she heard the sound of hooves over the planks. Emerging from the drifting fog, the Mather horses pulled into the farmyard. Florence was at the reins with Gran beside her. Apart from a large folded piece of canvas, a small keg, and several baskets piled high with dried bundles of herbs, the wagon bed was empty.

Thomas was just dragging the wool sacks out of the barn. Pa was standing in the yard waiting to meet the Mathers. Katie heard his voice half-muffled in the mist.

"Now, Gran," he said, "Katie told me you'd be along. We appreciate the offer, but it's not necessary for you to do our work." He peered into the wagon. "In fact, I've a better solution. Katie and I will take your herbs to Racine with our wool."

Gran Mather looked him in the eye. She took hold of the oak staff she always carried with her. "Andrew McEachron," she said. "Florence and I are going to market this day. We are most pleased to take Katie and the wool."

Gran turned to Katie's brother. "Thomas, load those sacks into the wagon, will 'ee?" She lifted her chin. "Else I will get down and load them myself."

Katie had never heard anyone cross Pa like that. Thomas glanced at his father.

Pa blinked. Then he shrugged.

"Very well," he said. "We've plenty of work in the fields once the fog burns off." He turned to the porch. "Fetch your journal, Daughter. You must keep an accurate record."

"Yes, Pa!" Katie dashed into the house, clattered up the stairs, and pulled her journal from under the mattress. When she got back outside, she saw the marshal ride into the yard.

"Good morning to you, Marshal," said Pa. "What brings you out our way?"

"Just keeping an eye on the county," Marshal Carter answered. "What's in the wagon?"

"Wool. Fine Merino wool. We're sending it to market."

Marshal Carter dismounted and walked over to the wagon. He reached into the bed and shifted one of the neatly piled sacks. "How many sacks have you?"

"Eight," said Pa. He sounded puzzled. Gran was suddenly occupied with adjusting her lace cap and did not meet his eye.

"Well, I'll leave you to it," said the marshal. "Good day, Mister McEachron, ladies."

He mounted his horse and trotted back toward the Mather Inn.

Katie did not dare look at Florence or Gran as she climbed up into the wagon. The keg placed among the baskets up front was to be her seat for the journey. Pa tied down the canvas to keep the high-piled sacks secured inside the wagon. Katie watched carefully as he knotted the ropes.

At last he turned to her. "Daughter, take heed of Gran on the journey. Be careful at the market. And keep a good account."

"Yes, Pa."

Pa handed Katie a small bag of coins. He said to Gran, "The McEachrons will take care of the tolls."

"That's right kind of 'ee, Andrew," Gran said.

Pa slapped the near horse on the hindquarters. "Safe travel then. We'll watch for you this evening."

Once the wagon passed Grace and Will's place and the Caswell homestead, Katie said the words she had been bursting to speak. "Was it Mister Banvard who brought the fugitives to you?" She was half-standing next to the keg to bring her face right up behind the two on the wagon seat. Florence clucked to the horses, urging them to pick up speed.

Gran turned to look at Katie. "It's not a matter to be discussed. The fewer who know, the safer for all."

"Have you been running slaves all summer?" Katie asked, raising her voice to be heard above the sound of trotting hooves.

"No," Gran said. "And we're doing no such thing now. We're easing their journey. 'Tis the way of the road."

Katie saw Florence and Gran glance at one another. Katie slumped down onto the keg. "You didn't mean to ask for my help, did you?" she said. "You didn't want me along on this trip."

Gran Mather turned to Katie again. This time her voice was gentle. "The Maker often sends help unbidden," she said. "Ours is not to question, but to use what's been given." Florence turned to smile briefly at Katie.

"There's a fine for helping slaves. A thousand dollars! A sign says so in Pa's office," said Katie, suddenly realizing the enormity of what they were doing.

"We don't wish to put our neighbors at risk," said Gran Mather. "We'll drop 'ee off at Ives Grove."

"Oh, no, you won't!" said Katie. "You might need my help before the day is through."

Well beyond The Rise, the road sloped down to the south branch of the creek. On a clear day, one could see almost a mile ahead on the roadbed above the marshy lowland. This morning the fog lay so thick Katie could barely make out the trees that marked the line of the creek.

"What if they haven't yet come?" she asked.

"Then I might take a notion to gather some blue flag," said Gran. "And we will water the horses here rather than stop at Ives Grove."

Florence slowed the team as they neared the creek and led them off the planks onto the dirt lane, then off the road bed entirely. Katie braced herself against the sides as the wagon lurched down the slope. With a jangling of harness, the team halted.

At a rustle in the reeds along the bank, Katie glimpsed a green kerchief. Hannah was peering out at Gran.

Gran glanced up and down the road. "Katie," she said, "untie the canvas. Florence, take the horses to water."

As Katie tugged at the knots, Florence led the horses to the edge of the creek. Gran checked the road again. "The way is clear," she said, motioning Hannah to come to the wagon.

Carrying Johnny on her hip, Hannah waded through the shallow water along the bank. "Miss Florence," she said quietly as she approached the horses, stepping lightly on the soft ground, "you best tromp over my footprints." Hannah boosted Johnny into the wagon and told him to lie down with the quilt for a pillow. Then she climbed nimbly into the wagon and squirmed almost completely under the wool sacks beside her son.

"Put them sacks right over top us," she said.

"But you'll smother," said Katie.

"Lean 'em across and leave space for breathin'."

Katie obeyed, burying the two in the wool before pulling the canvas back over and tying it down. "How are you? Can you breathe?"

"We's fine," came Hannah's muffled voice.

Florence climbed aboard and drove the wagon back onto the roadbed. When she reached a plank that extended beyond the others, she called "Gee!" to the horses. As the wagon bumped up onto the planked lane, Katie wondered what it must be like for the fugitives to feel the jolt and sway of the wagon from their hot and cramped hideaway.

The fog was lifting as the wagon neared Ives Grove. Gran pulled her staff from under the seat, and Florence drove in silence. Katie's stomach felt uneasy when she saw the tollgate just beyond the tavern. A number of teams and wagons and men stood about in the yard.

Abruptly the horses shifted their direction, their heads turning from habit toward the yard. "Gee there!" Florence said sharply, holding the horses to the road. As they neared the gate, Katie saw Mr. Ives standing next to the tollhouse.

The storekeeper called out, "Why, Miz Mather, what business takes ye on so fast?" Gran asked Florence to pull up the team. Mr. Ives strolled over to Gran's side of the wagon and stood with one hand on the sideboard.

"We're taking the McEachrons' wool to market," said Gran.

"That's right neighborly of ye," said Mr. Ives. "What else have ye got in the wagon?"

Katie could scarcely believe her ears. Did he suspect them already? "Nothing but herbs!" she said. From the basket beside her she lifted a fragrant sprig of rosemary. To her astonishment Mr. Ives reached over and took the sprig.

"My dear Miz Mather," he said, holding the rosemary like a nosegay, "are ye sure ye're not hiding a pasty or two?"

On the wagon seat Gran turned her whole body toward the storekeeper. Her grip tightened on her staff. "Mister Ives," she said, "I'll thank 'ee to stand back from my wagon."

"Now I'm certain ye've got some savory or sweet among your wares," he said. With his free hand he reached over the side and grasped the canvas.

Gran Mather's staff thwacked him just above the ear.

With a yelp Mr. Ives retreated, clutching his balding head. "What in God's name, woman! Are ye mad?" The rosemary lay on the planks at his feet.

"I asked 'ee to stand back," Gran said calmly, laying her staff across her lap. "Katie, pay the toll, will 'ee? Florence, please drive on."

The wagon was nearly a quarter-mile further down the road before Katie spoke. "You've quite an arm with a walking stick, Gran," she said admiringly. "I've a mind to begin carrying one myself."

"Comes a time when one must lay aside manners for a greater good," said Gran, "but such times are rare indeed." She tucked her staff back under the seat. "Five miles to the next tollgate."

Because the Mather wagon was more heavily laden, an approaching wagon rolled down onto the dirt lane to give Florence and her team the right to the planks. Though the driver touched his hat to them, Katie was too nervous to call a greeting, and neither Gran nor Florence even nodded to him.

Gran looked up and down the road. "You might pull back the canvas and shift a sack to get them some light and air till the next homestead."

Katie tugged at the knots and shifted the woolsacks to reveal the faces of Hannah and her son. Johnny tried to wriggle out, but his mother held him firmly. In frustration he dropped his head to the tightly rolled quilt.

"Never you mind," Katie said. "I'll come down there myself." She sat down among the baskets and wool sacks. "That's a fine quilt."

"Young miss's Mam, she give it to me."

Katie ran her hand over the squares of green and blue-gray. "This pattern is called Trip Around the World. That's a fine one for you travelers."

Propping her elbows on the floor of the wagon, Hannah said, "Miss Katie, what's a pass tea?"

"Pass tea?"

"The gen'lman that got whupped, he reckon you all were hidin' a pass tea."

Florence laughed. "*Pasty*. You heard him looking for *pasties*. Cornish pies."

"Katie, fetch them each one from that basket, will 'ee?" said Gran.

"You must have been more frightened than we were," said Katie. "Not knowing he was only looking for food."

"My body's done used to bein' scared," Hannah said, resting her hand on Johnny's head. "I jes' touch Johnny's face, and he knows to close his eyes and keep silence, 'cause Mama's prayin'."

"Did you pray when Mr. Ives was looking for pasties?" asked Katie.

"Yes, miss. I pray we be safe—me and Johnny and you all. I pray the Lawd keep watch over us."

"'Tis a dangerous road 'ee have come," said Gran, "one that needed many a prayer. Where did that journey begin?"

Hannah swallowed a bite of pasty. "Missouri, ma'am. Young master, he about to marry a wife from further south. Talk was, some of us was to be sold down there. I feared for me and Johnny—feared we might be split up."

She looked at her son, who was making short work of his pasty. He paused just long enough to flash a grin at her before taking another bite. "My Johnny still know how to smile," Hannah said, "but he pret' near old 'nough to start in the fields.

When young 'uns turn field hand, they too weary to smile at end of day."

"I hear things around the place," she went on. "I find out which way to the river. And which steamer captain don't look too hard for what he don't want to see. We hide in a big boat comin' up the great river."

"The Mississippi?" Katie said. "But how did you know when to get off the boat? How did you know where to go next?"

"Don't know much, Miss Katie, 'cept to go north. Late one night a porter help us sneak aboard another boat. Now we's going up a new river—the Rock, he call it. On boats, off boats, crossin' fields and forests. We gets powerful tired and hungry. Folks help us along the way—'go to this house, take some food, wait here, hide in the cellar.' Sometimes we wait and nobody come, so we head on ourselves. But all the time we pray the Lawd to guide us."

"One night a man row us up another river, the Fox. We gets a fine meal in a washhouse 'long the bank, and a gen'lman show me a map of all the places we been. St. Louis. Moline. Janesville. Rochester. I say the words over and over. Every night I whisper the names to Johnny before we says our prayers. My boy know how he come to freedom."

"Let me write that down for you."

"No need, Miss Katie. Scratches on paper don't mean nothing to me. Anyway, them words is forever in my heart."

"Soon's I learn my letters," said Johnny, "I's going to put Mama's words on paper."

Katie was embarrassed. Of course slaves were not taught to read. She wrote two lines in her journal and carefully tore out the page. "We're the last stage of your journey, Miz Hannah." She pressed the folded paper into the woman's hand.

"Katie," said Gran. "Cover them up now. Another tollgate is just ahead."

Katie paid the toll. As the wagon passed the first clusters of houses, she noticed that even Gran was sitting stiffly in the seat. Gran's eyes scanned the people and buildings and wagons ahead and alongside. Florence, too, was tense and silent.

Katie half-stood behind them, bracing herself against the back of the seat. Somehow she knew that this was not a time to keep silence. "Florence, do you remember the time we saw the Plains Indians camped in Racine, right in Haymarket Square? That was in 1845, wasn't it? Pa told us they were going to take those buffalo all the way to England."

Florence nodded. "That was my first memory of Lake Michigan. Granfer told me it was like the ocean, for one could look out to where the water turns to sky."

Gran smiled. "What was it my Abel said? 'Faith 'n' truth, even in this free country, man and beast alike will sail at Her Majesty's bidding.'"

Florence looked thoughtful. "I wonder whether those buffalo were ever truly happy in Queen Victoria's parks."

"I wonder how they fed them aboard ship," said Katie.

"I expect they fared better than many a soul who's come across the waters," mused Gran.

"Follow the street along the river," she instructed Florence. "We'd best not pass through Haymarket Square till we've made our delivery."

Katie was about to ask, "What delivery?" when she realized that Gran meant the fugitives. The city of Racine seemed suddenly to press around Katie, buildings on either side, streets crowded with wagons and buggies and passers-by. Anybody they met could be an enemy. How would they get safely through the mass of people?

Suddenly Katie recognized a face in the sea of strangers. "It's Charlie Doane!"

Her eyes grew round as Charlie turned at the sound of his name, smiled, and began to walk toward the wagon.

Chapter 17

The Warehouse

"Good day, Gran, girls," Charlie said. He stepped close enough to lean his hand against the canvas-covered rim of the wagon bed. "So, Gran, what brings you to Racine?"

He actually patted the canvas. "I thought the McEachrons would be bringing wool to market, not you."

Katie had a sudden impulse to pull out Gran's staff and thwack him across the head. Instead she sat as if frozen, hardly daring to breathe.

Then Gran did indeed pull her staff out from under the seat. "Why, Charlie," she said with a smile, "what good fortune has brought 'ee here!" Handing him the staff along with her satchel, she said, "Carry these for me, will 'ee?"

Quite ably, Gran climbed out of the wagon and tucked her arm through the crook of his elbow. "John asked that I look over some wares for the inn, and I need a man's advice. Come along now."

Katie and Florence stared at one another in dismay.

As she steered Charlie away, Gran called behind her, "Florence, mind 'ee make that delivery for me. Just tell them that 'ee are friends of a friend. We'll meet later by the wool merchant in the square."

Katie climbed over the wagon seat and sat beside Florence.

"Katie, when will 'ee learn to keep still?"

"I'm sorry," said Katie. "I was just startled to see Charlie." She paused. "I hope Miz Hannah is praying now," she whispered. "Do you know where to make . . . the delivery?"

Florence closed her eyes. A few long moments passed.

When she opened them, she said, "The Dutton warehouse. Gran said we were going to the Dutton warehouse! But I don't know where that is."

"Dutton? A. P. Dutton?" said Katie. "It's the first warehouse on the south pier."

Florence stared at her. "However do 'ee know that?"

"There's an advertisement on the wall by Pa's desk. I seem to spend a lot of time sitting there," said Katie. "Generally because I haven't kept still."

Florence gazed at her a moment more, and then laughed out loud. Katie grinned back, and Florence clucked to the team and headed toward the south pier.

The warehouse with A P Dutton neatly lettered above a wide door stood tall and dark against the bright sky. Florence pulled the team up in front of the building.

Katie wondered what they should do next. A man came out of a small side door. "How may I be of service to you?"

"We're friends of a friend," said Florence, "with . . . a delivery."

The man nodded. "I'll open the big doors. You can drive right in."

The man slid open the huge door to expose the dark interior of the vast building. As Florence drove the wagon into the warehouse and the door rolled shut behind them, Katie was momentarily blinded. She fought panic until her eyes adjusted to the dim light.

The warehouse was crowded with large wooden barrels and crates stacked about. A well-dressed man appeared at

Florence's side. "I don't often have young ladies delivering goods," he said. "Do you have a special parcel for me?"

Katie and Florence glanced at one another.

"Yes, sir," Florence said, after Katie's encouraging nod. "They're . . . the parcel is under the wool."

He nodded. "You've arrived just in time. The *Madison* sails at two."

"For Canada?" asked Katie, wondering whether she was talking to A. P. Dutton himself.

The man nodded. "We're loading the last of the cargo now." He looked in the back of the wagon and laughed. "Don't worry. You've come to the right place. You might let your passengers catch a breath of air before we stow them away."

In a flash, Katie hopped over the seat and unknotted the ropes, allowing Hannah and Johnny to squirm out from among the sacks of wool.

"Welcome to Racine, ma'am," the well-dressed man said to Hannah. "We must get you into a crate. Your ship awaits." He helped the woman down from the wagon, then put up his arms for Johnny. "Come along, young fellow."

Katie realized suddenly that the two people whom she had met only this morning were about to disappear from her life forever. She jumped out of the wagon and knelt to embrace Johnny, then extended her hand to his mother.

Hannah set down her bundle to take Katie's hand in both of hers. "Praise be that we have come this far."

"May 'ee reach safe haven," said Florence. She broke off a sprig of rosemary and held it out to Hannah. "For remembrance."

"Bless you both, young misses."

The last that Katie saw of the fugitives was a grin and a wave from Johnny, as Hannah's green kerchief sank into the crate.

Well before the wagon entered Haymarket Square, Katie could hear the clopping of hooves and jangling of harness, the squawking of poultry, the voices of farmers hawking their goods–vegetables and eggs, hay, wheat and wool. The square was flanked by the courthouse, a church, the Racine House Inn, and other businesses.

A multitude of horse teams and wagons ringed the edges. Katie thought she had never seen such confusion or heard such noise.

Florence stopped the wagon near a wool merchant.

"Sir," Katie said, raising her voice to be heard above the din, "I've fine wool to sell."

The wool merchant cocked his head. "Have you indeed? Let's see what you've brought, missy."

Katie handed him the sample she had pulled from the sack. She watched him rub the fleece between his fingers, pull a few strands, and give it an experimental twist.

"I'll give you twenty-five cents a pound," he said.

"Twenty-five cents!" Katie said. "Do you think I wouldn't know nails from oats? Look at the length of that staple! This is fine Merino wool, and it will cost you fifty cents a pound!"

"Not a buyer in the square will pay fifty for your wool. I'll give you thirty."

"Forty-five."

"I admire your spirit, missy. Will you settle for forty?"

"Sold," said Katie. "Now we'll unload. But mind you, I'll be watching as you weigh."

August 24, 1852
Sold to Mr. Hiram Walker
96 lbs. wool at 40c per pound
$38.40

Katie had just finished recording the transaction when she heard Florence cry out, "There's Gran!" Florence ran to embrace her grandmother, with Katie close behind.

Gran looked at the wagon. "Have 'ee made that delivery?"

"Indeed we have," said Katie. "Florence knew where to go, and I knew how to get there. And she remembered just what to say and . . . and what did you do with Charlie Doane?"

Gran and Florence smiled at Katie. "Never mind that," said Gran. "Let's sell our herbs and take our meal beside the shore."

Seagulls soared and dipped above the long line of ships docked in the harbor.

"Must be more than fifty ships out there," said Katie, looking out over the great expanse of Lake Michigan, dotted with long masts everywhere. "And the water turns to sky just like your Granfer said."

"Look at the names of the schooners," said Florence. "The *Zephyr* and the *Ohio* and the *Pride of America.*"

A bell rang once, twice, from the church on Haymarket Square. Katie and Florence stood hand in hand to look out past the busy docks, eager to catch sight of the *Madison* with its special cargo shipping out of the harbor.

August 24, 1852

Pa promised my journey to Haymarket Square would be a learning experience. He has no idea how right he was.

Florence and I are good friends once again.

How wonderful and strange that what broke us apart and what brought us back together all happened in Strawberry Glen.

I don't know whether I should even record the events that

brought us together, but if I don't, I shall burst.

I dare not tell a soul what Florence and Gran Mather and I have done this day.

So I shall tell my story here. . . .

Chapter 18

Harvest

Every morning in mid-September after the early milking and egg-gathering chores, Florence helped her mother and Gran fry bacon and potatoes and bake biscuits and stir gravy for more than thirty farmers and teamsters, who ate in shifts in the dining room. Those most eager to get on the road waited at the doorway of the kitchen to be handed a tin plate and a mug.

Afterward, Mrs. Mather washed up the last of the dishes and Gran made pasties in the cabin. Florence swept the dining room and the porch, looking out at the long lines of wheat-laden wagons passing the inn on the plank road, all heading east toward the harbor.

After the noon meal was served, Florence carried freshly aired blankets upstairs, where an elaborate system of canvas partitions divided the ballroom into sleeping quarters. Florence counted floorboards as she set out the bedrolls along the wall. Mrs. Mather prided herself on allotting guests a generous five planks during harvest.

"Florence!" came her mother's voice from downstairs. "I've asked Father to harness the wagon. If we make haste to Ives Grove, we can return before tea."

Florence could not remember the last time that she and her mother had driven out alone together. She dropped the last bedroll and hurried down to the kitchen.

Gran set a covered basket on the table. "Do give these to Mister Ives . . . with my compliments."

Mrs. Mather looked puzzled. "'Tisn't good business to give away what we've always exchanged in trade."

Gran smiled. "Poor Mister Ives had enough of our trade last month."

Florence drove the wagon while her mother sat stiffly beside her in her best bonnet, hands folded in her lap. "With a run of fine weather," Mrs. Mather said, "we'll have thirty men overnight, at a dollar each, for perhaps another week."

As the wagon rolled past The Rise, Florence only half listened to her mother's need to plan aloud. In the other half of her mind, Florence was remembering the last time she had traveled this road. How different the world had looked on that day when every neighbor and every stranger had seemed a threat.

Florence had to rein in the horses as they descended the long slope toward the bridge where the blue flag grew.

"Is this the place?" Mrs. Mather said abruptly.

Florence nodded. "They were hiding just there among the reeds."

"The Maker keep them," Mrs. Mather was quiet for a time after the wagon crossed the bridge, her calculations forgotten for the moment.

When the wagon pulled up outside the store, Mr. Ives was standing near the porch. He took off his hat and mopped his ruddy brow. "Ye've not brought that wildcat of a granddam, have ye?"

Mrs. Mather said, "Why Mister Ives, I can't think what 'ee mean."

Florence hid her smile and offered the basket. "Gran sent these with her apologies, sir."

Mr. Ives harumphed loudly. "So long as she's not packed any cudgels among the pasties."

Inside the store Mrs. Mather placed her orders and kept a sharp eye on the storekeeper as he measured and weighed and counted. As Mr. Ives loaded the wagon, she called Florence over to the fabrics and notions.

"'Tis time 'ee had a dress befitting a young lady," she said. "We could borrow Grace's pattern. What think 'ee of these fine woolens?"

Florence ran her hands over the various colors and pulled out a bolt of deep green, the color of oak leaves in summer.

"I'm partial to green myself," Mrs. Mather said. "We'll make that dress in time for the county fair."

When the wagon pulled into the Caswell smithyard, no one was about. Even the smithy was empty.

"Oh, they're all threshing at the Waites' farm," Florence remembered after she knocked on the Caswells' door.

Mrs. Mather was still in the wagon. "We'd best take the mail over there ourselves. Come along."

Florence remained standing at the gate. "I've one more call to make."

Mrs. Mather riffled through the sheaf of letters. "I'll wait here."

Florence stepped through the break in the hedgerow into the churchyard. At first she felt strange without Gran beside her, but soon the deep peace of the place surrounded her. At Granfer's grave she knelt and said the Cornish words as well as she could remember. At each of the three little graves she did the same. When she rose, Florence saw her mother standing at the hedgerow. Arm in arm they walked back to the wagon.

"And now 'ee must let me drive," Mrs. Mather said. "I can be idle no longer."

At first glance, the threshing scene looked completely confusing, men and boys crossing paths and shouting instructions and waving hats. But as Old Man Caswell came to greet the Mathers, Florence saw that the neighbors were working together, each with his own job to do.

Roy Waite and Thomas McEachron were handling the team of draft horses that powered the machine, stepping forward on a great inclined treadmill. Thomas eased the animals through their unfamiliar task of walking uphill, but going nowhere. Amos stood beside the large threshing machine, made by the Case company, where several men were feeding sheaves of wheat into the churning machine that ate the bundles like a hungry beast.

The young Waite boys did their part, handing empty sacks and twine to their father, who filled the sacks with the golden wheat as it poured out of the bottom of the machine. Owen Caswell was part of the crew that hefted the heavy sacks onto their shoulders and carried them to a nearby wagon.

As the chaff spewed out of the other end of the machine, another crew used pitchforks to pile the golden straw. Now and again a hat waved to halt the process, until with a whistle and wave, the noise and movement resumed.

"Isn't that amazing?" Amos said at Florence's elbow. "Used to take us weeks to do the work that Mister Case's machine now does in a couple days. It's hard on the horses, though. I reckon someday we'll have a special engine to replace them."

Florence smiled. "And what will Thomas do then?"

When the Mather wagon returned to the inn, an elegant buggy stood at the watering trough behind a handsome matched pair. Mrs. Mather gasped. "Have 'ee ever seen anything so fine?"

She climbed down from the wagon and hurried up the steps into the dining room. Florence was still standing with the horses when her mother came back out to the porch. "There's nary a soul inside," she said. "Wherever can they be keeping such a guest?"

Mr. Mather's cheerful whistle came from the barn. "Welcome home," he called, appearing in the doorway. "I'll see to the horses."

"Whose buggy is that, Father?"

"That's Richard Ela's rig. He's having a dish o' tea with Gran."

"In the cabin?" said Mrs. Mather. "What is Gran thinking when we've our own parlor in which none but teamsters ever sit?"

Florence followed her mother across the yard and watched her march up the steps of the cabin. Mrs. Mather was about to open the door when a gentleman stepped out onto the porch, shiny black hat in hand. "Good afternoon," he said. "I'm Richard Ela, ma'am. We haven't met, but I own a factory in Rochester, and I employ David Banvard. Might you be the Lavinia Mather whose inn is known the length of the plank road?"

Mrs. Mather blushed. "Good day, sir."

Gran stepped out onto the porch, as Mr. Ela continued, "As I was telling your mother-in-law, I came to thank you ladies for the assistance you have given our cause. Banvard told me of the numerous times you have aided him."

"And where is he now?" Florence could not help but ask.

"As law-abiding as can be, for now. I've put him on the Milwaukee run, delivering fanning mills again." Mr. Ela smiled. "No more midnight parcels."

He looked directly at Florence. "According to your grandmother, it was your quick thinking that saved those travelers." His gaze included them all. "It is women such as the three generations of Mathers who will keep our cause alive."

Chapter 19

Taking Toll

Just outside the orchard at Grace and Will's home, Katie sat at a quilting frame with Ma, Matilda, Grace, Emma, and Mrs. Caswell. Lit by the warm September sun, the crimson fruits and green leaves shone brightly against the white background of the Strawberry Patch quilt.

"What a beautiful company quilt," Ma said to Grace. "However did you manage to run a household and also make a quilt your first summer? Our Will chose a fine wife."

Grace smiled. "This wife chose a fine husband," she said, "with a family so willing to help."

A dog's bark announced the approach of a wagon. "Owen's brought Gran Caswell," said Grace, rising from her chair. "I told her we'd be quilting today."

Owen helped his grandmother down from the wagon. He stood politely by as Gran Caswell praised Grace's handiwork. Then he looked at Matilda. "Are 'ee not making a quilt for the fair?"

Matilda said lightly, "Grace represents the family well."

Mrs. Caswell said, "Who's minding the smithy while you've gone a-calling?"

"Oh, I'm not gadding about," Owen said. "I've a letter to deliver to Miss Katherine McEachron." With a flourish he pulled an envelope from his vest pocket.

Now Matilda looked up. "Who would be writing to Katie?"

Katie stuck her needle carefully into the cloth and reached with both hands for the letter. She stared at the words:

Katherine McEachron
Yorkville, Wisconsin

in her own handwriting on the front of the roughly folded piece of paper that was the envelope.

Grace said, "Why don't 'ee open it?"

With unsteady hands, Katie unfolded the envelope. Dried bits of rosemary slid out from the paper onto the quilt, along with a square of faded green cloth.

Matilda stared at the paper. "Why, the paper's blank!" she said. "Nobody's written to you at all."

"Ma, may I go call on Florence?" Katie's voice was hardly more than a whisper.

Ma peered at her closely and said, "Mind you're back within the hour."

Katie folded the herbs into the bit of green cloth. She rose from her chair and tucked the envelope into her apron pocket. Calmly she walked away from the quilt frame, but by the time she reached the other side of the orchard, she was running as fast as she could. She flew through the farmyard and up across the pasture to the inn.

"Florence! Florence!" she cried as she stood panting among the oaks. "Florence! I've heard!"

Florence came away from the laundry tub. "What are 'ee talking about, Katie?" she asked, wiping her hands on her apron.

"I've had word from Hannah and Johnny!"

"But how would 'ee know?" Florence asked.

"I wrote down my name and the township," Katie explained. "And I folded the paper. And Hannah used it as an envelope."

Florence looked shocked. "How could 'ee?" she said. "What if they'd been caught?"

"But they didn't get caught. Don't you understand?" Katie pulled the envelope from her pocket and pointed to the Canadian stamp. Eagerly she unfolded the paper and pulled out the green scrap of cloth.

Florence shook her head, then smiled in amazement. "A quilt square," she said with sudden understanding. "Why, this means they made it. They truly made it!"

"And we're the ones who helped them to freedom!" cried Katie, taking hold of Florence's hands. Clutching Hannah's little square made of a green kerchief between them, they whooped and spun under the great oaks until Mrs. Mather and Gran both left their work to see the spectacle.

Sept. 15, 1852

We could hardly contain our joy at the news from Canada. Gran Mather almost dropped her walking stick and joined the dance. Mrs. Mather was more practical. She told us to come into the kitchen before the whole township heard the commotion.

We sat in the kitchen having tea and cinnamon twists. I laid the kerchief square on the table, and Mrs. Mather touched it with one hand, then put her other hand to her face and looked out the window. Florence put her hand over her mother's, and Gran put her hand over theirs. Then I put my hand on top, except that my fingers were covered with cinnamon and sugar.

Florence said, "'Tis the sign," and we all laughed.

But I'm not laughing now. I'm wondering whether I ought to tell Pa. Should I keep silence?

What if Pa finds out from Mr. Mather or Gran? As the justice of the peace, what would he have to do? I must seek guidance from someone I can trust.

Next morning Katie found Will in the orchard. He was picking apples, examining each one before setting it into the basket. He greeted Katie with a smile. "Have you come to help me pick?"

Katie reached up to pull an apple from the nearest branch. "Will, do you reckon it's ever right to keep a secret? Not a silly secret between friends, but something important. Perhaps a deed, something someone has done. Would you ever keep a secret from Grace or . . . or from Pa?"

Will looked at Katie. He gestured toward the basket. "Were one diseased apple placed among the others, the disease could fester and spread. I reckon a secret could fester like that. I'd not want a source of trouble between myself and someone I love." He took the apple from Katie's hand.

After Katie dried the last of the supper dishes and stacked them in the cupboard, she peeked into the study.

"Pa," she said, "may I talk to you?"

Pa tacked a notice about the general election on the wall. "I must talk to John Mather about using the inn as a polling place," he said, more to himself than to Katie. Turning his chair to face her, he smiled. "Yes, Daughter? What's on your mind?"

Katie slowly crossed the threshold and sat down in the

corner chair with a thump. At first she said nothing, only fidgeted while her father watched patiently. Then, she knew the time had come. She couldn't hold it in any longer.

"I reckon you ought to know what I did," she said, her words tumbling out. "It isn't anything I set out to do, but sometimes things happen, Gran Mather says, when the Maker has plans that we don't understand."

She took a deep breath. "At any rate, it's done and can't be undone, but perhaps you ought to know. In case anybody ever mentions it."

Pa studied her intently. "And exactly what is it that can't be undone?"

Katie pulled her journal out of her apron pocket. "It's all in here, right after the wool price. I've marked the pages for you."

Pa took the small book from her and eyed her flushed face again. "Perhaps you'd like to wait in the next room."

"Yes, Pa."

Katie joined the rest of the family in the front room and sat down to the spinning wheel. As she started the wheel turning, the words she had written went round and round in her head:

I don't know whether I should even record the events that brought us together, but if I don't, I shall burst.

I dare not tell a soul what Florence and Gran Mather and I have done this day. . . .

"Katherine," Pa called a little while later. "Please come here."

Amos looked up. "You in trouble again?"

Ma said, "Amos, that will do."

Katie entered the study and sat down again in the chair.

Resting the journal on his knee, Pa looked at her a little while. Katie could not read his face.

"Well," he said at last, "I know now why Gran Mather was so insistent on taking our wool to market."

"Yes, Pa."

"Daughter, you broke the law of our country," he said. "A law that as justice of the peace I am sworn to uphold."

"Yes, sir," she mumbled, looking down into her lap.

"What you did was dangerous. Your action jeopardized the Mathers and your own family. On the record, I cannot condone what you did. Do you understand that?"

"Yes, sir," said Katie, still unable to look at him.

Pa reached over to tilt up her chin. "But off the record, Daughter, I'm proud of you."

"Truly, Pa?"

"Truly. Katherine, you traveled far on that trip to Racine. By your helpful actions, you have come to understand better the tragedy of slavery. Many in our community will not reach that destination for a long time."

"Can't we try to help them understand?"

"People must travel that road at their own pace. Yours was a short and easy journey. You are not descended from generations of family who have owned slaves. Nor does your family's livelihood depend upon the work of those enslaved."

"Pa, when I met Miz Hannah and Johnny, they looked so different from us. But Miz Hannah, she just wanted the best for her son, like you and Ma. And Johnny had a smile that could light up the night. I could just imagine him playing in the grass with Dan'l and Si Doane. He was just a little boy, Pa. Imagine Big Jim having to watch *his* grandsons being sold away! He would never allow it. I know that!"

"The time may come when Jim Doane is ready for such a conversation. However, at present you and I must keep silence on this matter. Do you understand?"

"I must not tell anyone else—not even Ma or Will or Matilda? And you're not going to arrest the Mathers or tell the marshal about Mister Banvard?"

"No, I won't. And, Daughter, you'd best keep your journal well hidden."

"Yes, Pa."

Katie returned to the front room, smiling as she sat down to the spinning wheel. Amos looked disappointed that nothing seemed to be wrong. Matilda and Ma were too intent on planning the threshing dinner to take notice of her.

A few minutes later Pa came into the room. "With the threshing machine coming tomorrow," he said, "I'll need Thomas and Amos on the crew." He turned to Ma. "As you and Matilda and Grace will be busy in the kitchen, I believe Katie should start at the tollgate."

The wheel stopped spinning. "Truly, Pa? May I take the tolls?"

"Thomas will be in the tollhouse overnight. I want you at the gate at sun-up. The wagons staying at the inn will be on the road early. You'd best get to bed."

"Yes, Pa. I'll do a fine job."

"I have no doubt of it."

The dew was thick on the grass the next morning as Ma and Katie walked to the tollhouse. Katie carried the last of her breakfast wrapped in a napkin—a couple of biscuits with jam. Thomas had already entered numerous tolls on the day's ledger.

"Hot biscuits and eggs in the kitchen, Thomas," Ma said. Thomas left the tollhouse quickly without a word.

"The toll prices are all listed," said Ma. "Sometimes one teamster will pay for a train of wagons, so you must multiply to calculate the toll. But I've heard you work sums as quick as Thomas. Remember that the amount of toll varies according to the number of animals pulling the wagon."

Katie nodded.

"When you receive a toll, record it in the ledger directly," her mother added. "Else you might forget when the next one comes along."

"Yes, Ma," said Katie. She had been taking toll in her mind for years and was quite comfortable with the operation. "I see two wagons coming out of the inn yard," she said.

"How much for their toll?"

"Two wagons, each pulled by two animals. Five cents apiece."

"Very good," Ma said. "I'll leave you then." She nodded toward the brass bell beside the ledger. "Ring the bell if you have any trouble or if the road gets too crowded."

"Yes, Ma," said Katie. "I'll be fine."

When the wagons arrived at the gate, Katie smiled at the first driver. "Good morning, sir. The toll is five cents."

"I've got his as well," he said, jerking his head toward the wagon behind and handing her a dime.

"Good day, sirs," Katie called as she swung open the gate and watched the wheat-laden wagons roll past.

Then she swung the gate shut and stepped into the tollhouse. She took the pen and neatly entered the amount in the ledger. Moving her pen to the bottom of the page, with a little flourish she wrote *Katherine McEachron*.

Report of Tolls received at Gate No. *4* ,
of Racine and Rock River Plank Road, for the
Week commencing and ending *Sept 12-18,* 1852 .

Subject of Toll

PASSENGER VEHICLES

drawn by 1 animal

   "   " 2 animals

more than 2 "

FREIGHT VEHICLES

drawn by 1 animal,

   "   " 2 animals | |

   "   " 3 "

   "   " 4 "

   "   " 5 "

   "   " 6 "

Horse, led or ridden,

Horses, Mules or Neat Cattle,

1-2 score Sheep,

1-2 "   **Swine,**

Total

Katherine McEachron, **Keeper**

Chapter 20

Fair Day

On the first day of the fair, Florence stood in the parlor. In her hands she had plumes of goldenrod and a fiery blaze of sumac leaves. She was arranging them in a pitcher, already bright with late Queen Anne's lace.

Mrs. McEachron had asked the Mathers to host the lady judges at the inn, and so Florence's mother was in a perfect frenzy, making the place habitable for her distinguished guests, who hailed from several neighboring counties.

Mrs. Mather peered in at the doorway. "In a day's time, those weeds will drop all over the floor."

Florence adjusted one stem. "In a day's time, I'll sweep the floor," she said, surprised at her own pertness. Out of the corner of her eye she watched her mother's face.

"Pick some posies for the freshening-up room, will 'ee? Mind 'ee use the best creamer."

Florence looked up in astonishment, but her mother had already disappeared. "Yes, ma'am!" she said to the empty air.

Later, Florence helped her mother serve tea to the lady judges, who sat with their printed lists of categories and tiny memorandum-books. One judge in a plumed hat told Mrs. McEachron, who had come to join the tea, about the merits of the Milwaukee Female College. "In these times," the lady said, her plumes nodding briskly, "we cannot allow the intellectual power of our young women to remain hidden away. Such gifts must be used for the benefit of our community."

Mrs. McEachron said, "We have some fine scholars here in Yorkville. Florence Mather is one of our best." She smiled at Florence. "Tell us more about what your school has to offer."

As the Milwaukee judge began to speak of the course of study, Florence stood tray in hand while Mrs. Mather lingered in the doorway.

After the noon washing-up, Florence and her mother walked across the inn yard past the log barn. Even though she had watched the preparations day by day, Florence was still astonished at her first sight of the Racine County Fair. The north end of the Doanes' front forty was lined with nearly a hundred wagons and buggies. The clamor of livestock provided a constant accompaniment to all the other goings-on.

Among the dozen enormous tents, Florence could pick out the dinner tent in which ladies of the Scotch Settlement church and the Methodist chapel were working together to feed hungry fairgoers. Next to the dinner tent stood a dance platform where a fiddler sawed a merry tune. Florence remembered someone's claim that there would be enough players that the music at the fair would never end.

Mrs. Mather led the way to the domestic skills exhibits, which were flanked by a brilliant wall of quilts swaying on a line strung between two tents. Florence and her mother saw woolen mittens and stockings, lace doilies, and silk bonnets.

They paused before a framed sampler of crewel embroidery featuring a road winding among fields and pastures with a house and barn in the distance. Below the scene were stitched the words of the Psalmist: *Yea, I have a goodly heritage.* From the tips of the ripening wheat in the foreground to the unmistakable silhouette of a burr oak in the pasture, every detail had been painstakingly rendered.

Mrs. Mather said, "This brings to mind the poem 'ee memorized for Recitation Day. What were the lines about two harvests, one for the farmer and one for the poet?"

Florence smiled.

> *A second crop thine acres yield*
> *Which I gather in a song.*

A little distance from the exhibit tents and the livestock pens, a line of tradesmen's booths stood among the oaks at the edge of the field. Florence and her mother passed a cobbler, a tin peddler's gaily-painted wagon, and a cooper with his staves and a pyramid of barrels. Next to the harness-maker's booth, they found the table of Owen Caswell arrayed with trays of nails, fittings, hooks, and hinges.

"Good day, neighbors," he said. "Florence, what think 'ee of the fair?"

"I did like to see the goods, but I find watching the fairgoers even more interesting."

Owen chuckled. "'Ee don't miss a thing, do 'ee?"

Mrs. Mather was starting to fret about being so long away from the inn. "Come, Florence," she said. "We'll see fairgoers in our own dining room soon enough."

"Might I borrow Florence for the afternoon?" said Owen. "I'd be much obliged if she'd mind the table as I step out now and again. My grandfather, bless him, can't help but gad about the fairgrounds."

Mrs. Mather straightened her bonnet. "Well," she said. "I expect we can manage till tea-time. And she will prove a good help to 'ee, Owen." She nodded and walked swiftly away.

Florence artfully arranged the hinges and brackets, candleholders and heart-shaped hooks. She enjoyed hearing the metallic jingle and clink as she counted out nails for customers.

Then a shadow fell across the tray of hinges. Florence saw Owen's jaw tighten slightly.

David Banvard was standing before the table. For what seemed a long moment, the two men eyed one another in silence.

Owen was the first to speak. "A good afternoon to 'ee," he said.

"And to you." The teamster held up an iron object in one hand. "I'm in need of advice," he said.

Owen took the ironwork, which Florence recognized as a broken wagon hasp, and examined it in his strong and capable hands. "I've no forge here," he said. "Have 'ee brought this wagon to the fair?"

Banvard shook his head. "I rode here," he said.

Owen looked up from the broken hasp. "On that fine sorrel?" he asked.

Florence saw something like a smile cross the teamster's face. "On Fancy," he agreed.

Owen's hands pressed the broken pieces together expertly. "Jim Doane will be glad to hear that," he said. "Will 'ee race on the morrow?"

David Banvard shrugged. "I'm not much for a contest," he said. His eyes never left Owen's.

The blacksmith was the first to look away, and Florence had the sense that Owen Caswell had forgotten she was even standing there. He turned the broken hasp over and over in his hands. Then he looked at Banvard again. "Nor am I," he said. His voice was oddly tentative. "She's a beauty," Owen said.

"That she is," said the teamster, "and with spirit to match." Now David Banvard was the one who looked away. His long fingers played with the box of nails on the table between them. He lifted a handful of nails. "Owen Caswell," he said, "I look to you to say whether I ought to stay the course."

The blacksmith set the broken hasp on the table. "Are 'ee in it for the long run?"

The teamster's hands grew still. "For all my life."

Owen picked up the broken hasp and held it as if weighing it. When at last he spoke, Florence barely recognized the low voice of the man who could sing the old ballads so well. "Then I can think of no reason for 'ee not to try."

Banvard pushed back his long dark hair, and his face was alight with a kind of wonder. "A good day to you, Owen Caswell," he said. He turned and disappeared into the crowd.

"And good luck to 'ee, David Banvard," the blacksmith murmured. His hands still cradling the broken hasp, he bowed his curly head.

From her corner Florence blinked hard as she felt a prickle of tears.

Chapter 21

The Front Forty

October 5, 1852

For all I have longed to take the tolls, I wish I had not done so today. Such a number of wagons and buggies bound for the fair! Farm wagons laden with produce, and fancy buggies carrying the city folk. One family must have been on the road since daybreak, for they said to me, "You're mighty lucky to live so close!"

"Lucky?" says I. "Who is going to the fair and who is minding a tollgate?" A little boy in the wagon looked sad, until I laughed and assured him I would go to the fair on the morrow.

The whole neighborhood is talking of Grace's prize-winning quilt, but the Strawberry Patch pattern was my idea. Still, I will hold my tongue. It would be unseemly for me to speak of it.

"Ma!" Katie asked the next morning as her mother poked her with a hairpin. "Whatever are you doing?"

Her mother set down the hairbrush. "Go see for yourself." She followed Katie to the looking-glass in the front room.

"Oh, Ma!" Katie whispered. "Will it stay?" Her mother had coiled her braids and secured them tightly round her head.

"It will fare best if you leave your bonnet in place," her

mother said. Katie's gaze never left the glass as she slipped her shawl around her shoulders. Matilda entered the room wearing her sky-blue calico. Her hair was done up carelessly, and she did not even notice Katie's new style.

When Katie stepped outside the air was crisp, and sunlight played among the bright leaves. Already the plank road was busy with traffic headed for the Doanes' fields. Pa stopped at the tollhouse for a quick word with Mr. Shephard, who had been hired to mind the gate. As the McEachron family walked down the dirt lane next to the plank road, their steps quickened as they passed the log barn of the Mather Inn and saw the fairgrounds laid out before them.

"It's as if a city has sprung up on the front forty!" Katie said. "Or an enormous Haymarket Square!"

"Andrew McEachron!" A man whom Katie recognized as one of the other county supervisors approached and greeted Pa. The two of them began to talk, then Pa excused himself from the family and accompanied the fellow toward the tents.

Ma glanced around. "See the dinner tent yonder?" she said. "Matilda and I will be working till after the noon hour. The three of you are to meet us there when the midday crowd has eased." She looked them over and reached out a hand to smooth Amos' unruly hair. "Stay together and mind your manners." She and Matilda disappeared into the crowd.

Katie turned this way and that, unable to decide where to look first, but Amos knew exactly what he wanted to do. "Reckon we ought to start with the machines," he said to Thomas. "I've a mind to have a closer look at Mister Case's thresher."

As her brothers discussed the workings of various designs of threshers and reapers, fanning mills and corn shellers,

Katie admired the fancy lettering and scrollwork on the finest machines.

In the livestock tents, they saw sheep and cattle and hogs and poultry. In the produce tent, they found Will's half peck of apples with a premium ribbon attached. Pumpkins and carrots, beets and onions were among the harvest display. At the grain exhibit, Katie admired the golden sheaves of wheat before she was whisked off to see the horses.

When at last Katie and Amos managed to pull Thomas away from the hitching rails and bring him to the church dinner tent, they found Ma and Matilda and Grace washing dishes. Now that the crowd had eased, there was plenty of room at the rows of plank tables, and Pa and Will soon joined them. The McEachron women served up platters of fried chicken, cornbread, and green beans, and then sat down themselves to enjoy the meal.

"We fed nearly five hundred people," said Ma. "We could scarcely keep up with the washing."

"I've seen almost everybody I ever met in my life," said Matilda, wearily pushing back some of her escaping hair.

"And now," Ma said when they all finished eating, "I am ready to see the fair. Let's begin with that quilt of yours, Grace."

Katie followed Ma, Grace, and Matilda to the displays of domestic goods. Among the bright quilts swaying between the tents Katie saw a Trip Around the World, Log Cabin, and several album quilts. Even from afar, the red and green Strawberry Patch pattern was the most distinctive. Katie touched the silky premium ribbon pinned to one corner, proud to have shared in the making of it.

"I daresay there's more than one way to preserve strawberries." said a voice behind her.

Katie turned to see Florence standing beside Gran Caswell.

Gran Caswell gave Grace's hand a little squeeze, happy to see her granddaughter. "At the inn, Florence heard the judges talking of this quilt," she said. "They remarked on–what said 'ee, Florence?–the charming originality of the design. Now come along, Senator White is about to give his address."

At the edge of the crowd Katie stood between Florence and Grace, rising on tiptoe to get a better view. Pa himself was on the speakers' platform with the other two county supervisors. Next to him was Mr. Ela, whom Katie recognized from Independence Day. The other man must be Senator Philo White.

"Ladies and gentleman," the senator began with a great booming voice, "I welcome you to the first Racine County Agricultural Society Fair." His words rang out over the crowd. "I know that today you have seen the finest livestock in Racine County. You have seen the finest fruits of your neighbors' labor in the fields and gardens. You have seen the machines that make possible the harvest of that bounty, fine inventions by men of vision, designed and manufactured right here in Racine County.

"And," he said with a flourish of his hand to point across the fields, "I believe that today most of you traveled here on the Racine and Rock River Plank Road, another proof of the great vision of the good people of Racine County, to make a road that allows us to transport our goods to the harbor and share our bounty with the world!"

Katie clapped and cheered with the crowd.

"And I say to you today," Senator White continued, "that I have traveled to Janesville, where I have taken in the sights of our own grand State Fair. But even there, my friends, I saw nothing that could rival what I have seen on these fine fairgrounds this very day!" The applause was deafening.

The senator held up a hand to quiet the crowd. "Now, on behalf of the Wisconsin State Agricultural Society, I have been asked to present this medallion to Richard Ela of Rochester. Mister Ela, please accept this token of our appreciation for your many contributions to the progress of Wisconsin."

Mr. Ela graciously accepted the bronze medal. One of the county supervisors said a few words of thanks and added that the horse racing would begin at three o'clock. As the crowd began to disperse, Katie pushed toward the platform to greet Pa.

Florence followed her, and suddenly the girls found themselves standing in front of Mr. Ela himself. He nodded kindly to Katie and then looked at Florence. "Good day, Miss Mather."

"And good day to 'ee."

Mr. Ela glanced from Katie toward Pa and back again. "Might you be Miss Katherine McEachron?"

"Yes, sir."

"I'm pleased to make your acquaintance, Miss McEachron," he said. "I've heard fine things of you."

Katie remembered to say, "Thank you, sir." She smiled up at Mr. Ela. "I've heard fine things of you as well."

As Katie and Florence and Matilda stopped at a lemonade stand, the little Doane boys came running over to greet them, their grandmother just behind them. Si stared wide-eyed at Katie. Daniel frowned and said, "You look all grown up."

Mrs. Doane chuckled. "Land's sake, of course she's growing up." She nodded. "Turning out right nice, too."

Matilda glanced at Katie with amusement, but then her face changed as she looked out past the boys. Just beyond the lemonade stand stood David Banvard. Katie had not seen him since the morning many weeks ago he had left the inn yard with slave catchers on his trail.

Heedless of Matilda's attempt to restrain her, Katie charged through the crowd to him. "Mister Banvard!" she called. "Mister Banvard!" She arrived at his side breathless, only then remembering that she could say nothing to him about what had happened during that day when Hannah and little Johnny had passed through their lives.

The lanky teamster smiled down at her. "Good day, Miss Katie," he said. "Are you and your sister enjoying the fair?"

"Oh, yes," Katie said.

Katie and the teamster strolled back to Florence and Matilda. Mr. Banvard bowed slightly, hat in hand. "I wish you a good day, Miss McEachron."

Matilda's chin was high and her cheeks were bright. "I did not look to find you here." Her voice was as cold and tart as lemonade.

The teamster pushed back his dark hair. With just a hint of a smile he said softly, "Then where did you look to find me?"

Big Jim Doane approached carrying two glasses of lemonade, which he handed to his grandsons. Seeing the teamster, he said, "You there, Banvard," he said. "Is the weather cool enough for you today? What'll it take to get your sorrel onto my track?"

The teamster shrugged. "I'm well content, I thank you," he said.

Big Jim eyed the two of them. "How about a friendly wager?"

Mr. Banvard shook his head again. "I've nothing to wager but a broken wagon."

"I'll wager that wagon against–what is it you want? What would you have, man?"

The teamster glanced at Matilda. "I recall a quote I heard in conversation not long ago. 'Go where he will, the wise man is at home.'" Banvard looked back at Big Jim. "As I see it, all I've need of is a piece of land."

Big Jim took a step closer and planted his feet firmly. "I know of no better land than this," he said. "What say you to this land?"

"This land?"

"The forty acres under your feet. What say you to that, Banvard?" Big Jim's face was flushed with excitement.

"What do you mean, sir?"

Big Jim Doane stared at him a long moment. At last he spoke. "I'll wager that my Lightning can beat your Fancy. I'll wager your wagon against the right to buy this land, the forty acres upon which we stand. At a fair price, of course. What say you to that?"

Mr. Banvard looked about him, gazing past the open fields to the surrounding oaks. "That's a prize worth having," he said. "Who'll bear witness to this?"

"Andrew McEachron!" bellowed Big Jim. "We need a justice of the peace!"

At the oval track of trampled grass around the lone oak, men and horses moved restlessly. Some riders were trotting around the track to let the excitable animals work off some of their nerves. Others were leading their horses, casting an anxious eye back to watch the precise action of each hoof. Other men checked their tack, adjusting a bridle, tightening a girth.

Big Jim stood at Lightning's head, while Charlie sat in the saddle. Thomas and Amos were nearby, and all the boys from Yorkville had come to cheer on their township's favorite.

Only the teamster on the sorrel mare stood alone and apart.

Katie was pleased to see Mr. Mather and then Mr. Ela walk over and lay a hand on Fancy's neck and speak a few words to Mr. Banvard.

The president of the agricultural society stood at the start-and-finish line and signaled the contestants to take their places. The onlookers called words of encouragement as the riders lined up along the track.

Now Katie could see the faces of the horsemen clearly, but all of them seemed a blur, except for a grinning Charlie Doane and an unsmiling David Banvard.

With great deliberation, the president walked down the row of horses. He caught the eye of each rider in turn and got the nod.

Returning to his designated spot at the edge of the track, he raised his hat high.

"Ready, men? On the mark now. Steady . . . and GO!"

The hat swooped down, the horses sprang forward, and the crowd whooped and hollered.

In the first moments of flailing hats and galloping hooves, Katie could scarcely make out which horse was which. But then she caught sight of Charlie Doane whaling away at the powerful haunches of the chestnut.

On the far turn, she finally saw the flashing golden flanks of the sorrel. She was not at all surprised when those two horses pulled out ahead of the pack . . . Lightning in the lead, just a neck ahead of Fancy.

Katie had always cheered for the Doane horses, sharing the pride and affection of the neighborhood in Big Jim's love of good horses. She watched the two riders flattened forward against the streaming manes of the horses and listened to the cries around her, most cheering for Charlie Doane and Lightning.

Katie climbed up onto a nearby wagon tongue, cupped her hands around her mouth, and shouted, "Go to it, Fancy! Go to it, Mister Banvard!"

She saw her neighbors and her family turn to stare. Katie waved her sunbonnet high in the air. "Go, Fancy, go!"

Florence, too, began to cheer for Mr. Banvard. Then Matilda almost knocked Katie off the wagon tongue, jostling for a place and shouting, "Go to it, David, go!" Clinging to one another and shrieking, the McEachron sisters made quite a spectacle of themselves as the sorrel mare swept a moment later across the finish line, ahead by an impressive half a length.

Led by Mr. Mather and Mr. Ela, the crowd swarmed to form an admiring circle around Fancy and her rider. Charlie Doane dismounted and threw his hat to the ground in disgust. The little Doane boys stroked Lightning's muzzle in sympathy. Big Jim pushed back his hat and shook his head and muttered a few words Katie could not hear.

Later the settlers gathered at the dance platform, where the Yorkville musicians introduced a bass fiddler from Rochester and a banjo player from Racine. Old Man Caswell called, "Find a partner, will 'ee? Let's have a fine new American tune."

Katie watched the other fairgoers smiling and taking hands. Opal Doane led Charlie out to the floor, where Mr. Banvard was already standing opposite Matilda in the growing line of dancers. Behind her Katie heard Florence's clear voice: "Owen, would 'ee care to dance?"

Big Jim Doane was suddenly towering above Katie. He bowed politely. Then he gave a smile and shrugged his shoulders. "Quite a day for all, Miss McEachron. It would lighten my sorrow at losing the race today if I might have this dance."

As they joined the line, Old Man Caswell said, "There's the man we need to see. Big Jim, come up front here, will 'ee?"

He waved his fiddle bow. "Friends, here's one 'ee have to thank for this fine day. Jim Doane is a good neighbor and a generous friend. We're blessed indeed to know such as he!" As the crowd applauded, Big Jim nodded and waved his own thanks.

Then Old Man Caswell winked at Katie and struck up the opening bars of "Camptown Races."

Never before had Katie stood at the head of the line. She looked down the long rows of faces–old and young, native and foreign-born, townspeople and country folk.

She curtseyed to her partner, stepped forward in time to the music, and joined the dance.

October 6, 1852

I am writing by candlelight. Matilda is already long asleep.

All summer I looked forward to the fair, but I never imagined a day quite so eventful. My Strawberry Patch idea showed charming originality, Mr. Ela spoke well of me, and Mr. Banvard's Fancy earned him the Doanes' front forty. What a story could be made of the first Racine County Fair!

At the dance this evening, Mathers and Doanes and Caswells congratulated Mr. Banvard and welcomed him as a

new neighbor. Even Big Jim said, "At least I'll have a neigh-
bor with a worthy horse." Ma promised Mr. Banvard a purple
lilac next spring.

Perhaps someday the Front Forty might have a white one
as well.

How much has happened since the lilacs bloomed!

Pa once said that anything can happen between blossoms
and harvest. But to lose a friend and gain her back, to help a
family to freedom, to see all of Yorkville making merry—no one
could have imagined that.

I shall always remember 1852 as the Plank Road Summer,
when I journeyed from Lilacs to Wheat Sheaves.

Katie marked her page with a green square of faded cloth.
Then she tucked the journal under the mattress and blew out
the light.

Appendix A

To Our Readers

We Demuth sisters grew up on the old McEachron homestead in Racine County, Wisconsin. On a farm across the pasture, our neighbors lived in a large house that had once been known as the Mather Inn. During our childhood, we learned that the rural highway running past our house had been a well-known plank road over a hundred years ago. Older neighbors told us that lilac bushes near the road marked the location of a little tollhouse.

In the late 1840s, the Racine and Rock River Plank Road Company had "rolled out a carpet of planks" to encourage farmers to bring their wheat to the Racine harbor on Lake Michigan. During the harvest season, over a hundred loaded wagons traveled east on the plank road each day. Travelers paid toll at gates about every four miles. Inns accommodated farmers and teamsters overnight after each day's journey. However, by the mid- to late 1850s, newly-built railroads replaced the plank roads as a more efficient way to transport goods.

In our story we kept the names "McEachron" and "Mather," although the girls and their families are products of our imaginations. Still, some of the tales were based on fact. For instance, buffalo really were herded into Racine and shipped to England for Queen Victoria's parks.

We have no evidence that the McEachron or Mather families were involved in helping runaway slaves. However, according to local history, Richard Ela's washhouse along the Fox River in the village of Rochester was a haven for fugitive slaves. In Racine, A. P. Dutton used his warehouse to hide runaway slaves seeking ships. The steamship *Madison* is listed as one of the "floating stations" of the Underground Railroad which transported fugitives to Canada. Because the plank road was the quickest route from Rochester to the harbor in Racine, some runaway slaves would have made their way to freedom past the Mather and McEachron properties.

Southeastern Wisconsin has a long history of producing farm equipment. In 1852, Richard Ela received an award for his contributions to agriculture, and Jerome Case's threshing machines were the beginning of an enterprise that led to the worldwide fame of Case tractors and other agricultural machinery.

The first Racine County Fair was held just west of the Mather Inn in the early 1850s. Racine County residents must have been pleased to hear Senator Philo White praise their agricultural exhibits as superior to those at the State Fair in Janesville. Along with the exhibits, horse racing was recorded as one of the crowd-pleasing events of early fairs. In our own childhood, the Racine County Fair was a highlight of the year, though tractor pulls and demolition derbies had replaced the horse races. These days, when we are able to attend the Fair, we enjoy seeing old friends and celebrating the Yorkville community we remember well.

Appendix B

To Learn More

Further historical and educational resources on varied topics, including the history of plank roads and the Underground Railroad, are available online at the website:

www.plankroad.wordpress.com

We invite you to explore and share any comments you have about *Plank Road Summer*.